RETRIBUTION

POWELL BOOK 5

Bill Ward

"Man is the cruelest animal."
— Friedrich Nietzsche

CHAPTER ONE

1998

Bob Hale had not originally wanted to visit Zagreb, despite assurances he would have around the clock protection. It was 1998 and he was a Lawyer, working for the International Criminal Tribunal for the former Yugoslavia or ICTY as everyone referred to it, based in The Hague. When he joined twelve months earlier, he had expected to spend all his time in a smart office searching through evidence and preparing cases against individuals charged with war crimes. He certainly hadn't envisaged having to actually visit the scenes of the appalling crimes he was prosecuting.

He had only taken the job because he believed it would be good for his career and he was an extremely ambitious man. He hoped one day to go into politics and the experience of working for the ICTY would look very good on his CV.

Despite his initial protestations, Bob had finally been persuaded to visit Zagreb by a friend in the legal profession, who was aware of his special tastes and convinced him the benefits available outweighed any potential risks. Croatia had been ravaged by war and in the aftermath, many of the ordinary people were struggling to put food on their table. A little money would go a long way in Zagreb.

Bob was in the back of a dirty old car with worn leather seats on his way to sample some of those special benefits, at a secret address outside of the city. A smell of stale tobacco filled his nostrils and he passed the time gazing out of the window. The view was depressing, rather like his current mood, which had turned from early optimism at the outset of the journey, to deep concern he had made a foolish and possibly fatal decision.

Bob didn't feel like making conversation with the brute of a man who had picked him up from outside his hotel. Between the two of them, they probably had the right quantity of brawn and brain for any two people but the division had not been equal. Bob was all brain and zero brawn. A private school education, followed by a first class degree from Oxford University, was testament to the brain. A loathing of sports involving strenuous physical activity was only partially responsible for the lack of bulging muscles, like the man driving the car possessed. Bob was only five feet eight inches tall and had a naturally slim frame. The genetics had never been too conducive to brawn.

Bob had been quite specific about his requirements and the promise of having been found exactly what he wanted, had made him so excited, he had temporarily lost his mind. That was the only possible explanation for the madness that had led to him agreeing to take this journey. Back home in Brighton, he mostly had to settle for imitations of the real thing but today he was going to experience what his imagination had long desired. At least he would if he stayed alive long enough and if they hadn't lied.

They had driven for thirty minutes and he was dismayed to find himself in an unremarkable suburb dotted with large grey, concrete apartment blocks. The people on the streets looked equally as grey. The heat would have been welcome beside the swimming pool back at the hotel but in a car with no air conditioning, it was becoming unbearable. He loosened his tie and watched the children playing on the streets, who were kicking an empty tin can around as a football. There was poverty everywhere.

Bob was deeply concerned he could be the subject of a kidnap attempt and his life may be in danger. He had been foolish putting his trust in people he didn't know. In theory, he should be worth a great deal of money as a hostage but he remembered the induction, where he was warned kidnappers rarely returned their victims in one piece, even if the ransom was paid.

The man Bob had spoken with, who made today's arrangements, was clear there were no limits to what he could organise if Bob had enough money. Bob had reigned in his imagination once he heard the costs of fulfilling his immediate dream. There were other dreams that would have to remain unfulfilled for the time being.

Bob was sweating and frustrated. His mind was telling him that men who could obtain anything he wanted for the right price, wouldn't have any qualms about kidnapping a valuable lawyer. He was about to say something to the driver, when the car finally pulled to a halt in front of one of the rundown tower blocks.

"We are here," the driver announced in heavily accented English.

Bob forgot his concerns and focused on the excitement for what lay ahead. He stepped out of the car and followed the driver towards the building. He was disappointed by the surroundings but five star hotels weren't really suitable for what he had in mind. His mouth was dry from a combination of the heat and nerves. He would pay a lot of money right now for a drink of water.

An old, stooped woman with a face like well-worn leather pushed past them as they entered the building, causing the driver to swear. She had a scarf pulled tightly around her head and met the driver's angry words with a broad smile, revealing most of her front teeth were missing. Bob turned away from the woman's gaze, not wanting to be identifiable.

The lift was broken and the driver led the way up three flights of stairs. When the driver knocked on a door with no number they were immediately admitted inside.

"Welcome Mr. Hale," the man who had opened the door, greeted him as they stood in the small hallway. "I am Marko. I trust you had a pleasant journey."

"It was fine," Bob confirmed.

"Good. I believe you have something for me?"

Bob put down the bag he was carrying and reached inside his jacket. He took out an envelope. "A thousand dollars as agreed," he said as he handed over the envelope. He remembered the conversation where he had suggested paying in pounds and they had laughed. They only dealt in dollars.

Marko glanced inside the envelope but didn't count the money. He took out two notes and then placed the envelope inside his own jacket pocket. Bob wondered if the two notes, which added up to one hundred dollars was payment to the family. If so, they had been cheated but it wasn't his problem.

"Come with me," Marko said with a smile and led the way into a small living room. "Take a seat. Would you like me to bring you a drink?"

Bob remembered the warnings about drinking the tap water. "Do you have any alcohol?"

"Of course. I will bring you a Slivovitz. It is our national drink. I will be back in a minute"

"Thank you." Bob had already tasted Slivovitz in the hotel bar. It was plum brandy and had quite a kick.

He realised his driver had not followed him into the room so he was alone. He was looking out of the window when he heard the door open. He turned and couldn't help the smile that crossed his face. Any moment now the adventure would begin.

The woman who followed Marko into the room was in her mid-thirties and had once been very attractive. Now her eyes looked tired and she didn't return his smile. She looked defeated by life. Bob wondered if she had lost her husband in the war. The atrocities committed in the war were beyond his comprehension. Men had behaved like crazed animals.

"Everything is ready for you," Marko said. "There is a bottle of Slivovitz waiting for you in the room. Go with this woman." He flicked his head to indicate Bob should follow the woman. "I will be waiting here for you. Take your time. There is no hurry."

Bob followed the woman out into the hallway. A door opened and a young boy stuck his face out. The woman said something sharply Bob didn't understand but the boy quickly disappeared back behind the door. The woman opened another door and led the way into a bedroom with a double bed and a single wardrobe. There was little space for anything else.

Bob was transfixed by the sight of the young girl sitting on the bed. He had been promised she was eleven years of age, a virgin and pretty. They hadn't lied. She was slim with long brown hair that framed a waif like face. She was wearing a simple red dress. Her eyes were staring down at the floor.

"This is Mia," the woman said without looking at the girl.

"Hello Mia," Bob said, placing a large brown, paper bag on the bed next to the girl. "I have a present for you."

The girl didn't move. Then he realised she probably didn't speak English and hadn't understood what he said. He turned back to the woman. "Please tell Mia I have brought her a present."

The woman said something in her native tongue and the girl looked up expectantly. Bob wondered if the woman was Mia's mother? Surely not.

Mia saw the bag and excitedly emptied the contents over the bed.

"Barbie," she exclaimed, lifting up one of the boxes. She examined the second box containing accessories for the doll.

Bob smiled broadly. He had found a universal language.

"I will leave you," the woman announced. She said something further to Mia in her language. "If you need anything, knock loudly on the door."

CHAPTER TWO

PRESENT

Powell was undecided about whether leaving the EU was a good or bad idea. Afina had tried to convince him it was important the UK remain but admitted she was mostly driven by self-interest as she was worried she would be made to leave the country, if there was a vote to exit.

Powell had joked that might be a good reason for him to vote to leave but Afina hadn't seen the funny side and he realised she was genuinely concerned. Several of his bar staff were from Eastern Europe and although he didn't believe people already living in the country would be kicked out, he decided to take the easy path and vote for the status quo.

In the end, his vote had not been sufficient to stop those in favour of leaving from winning, which had left Afina in a black mood for several days. She even doubted whether he had actually voted to remain as if his single vote had somehow made all the difference. At this point, he had become a little impatient and pointed out it didn't matter which way he had voted as those in favour of leaving had won by more than a million votes.

Powell's leg had fully recovered from being shot a few months earlier and wanting to take on some work, he had accepted a job on the staff of the local Member of Parliament, who was part of the government's team negotiating Britain's exit from the EU. This seemed to somehow confirm for Afina he had voted to leave, despite his protestations to the contrary.

It wasn't Powell's first choice of work but he had been asked by his friend Brian in MI5 as a personal favour and Powell owed him so many favours, he had little choice but to do as asked. Brian admitted he didn't know the man but in turn was doing a favour for someone else. Powell smiled at how the wheels of government turned and the establishment pulled together to help each other when necessary.

As there was no other work on the horizon and it was only a four week gig, Powell was recruited as an administrative assistant but everyone on the staff understood he was there as a bodyguard. Threats had been made to the MP but they weren't serious enough to merit official protection so Powell was being employed in a private capacity. Powell did wonder if he was called an administrative assistant so his cost could be claimed as some form of expense. Since the revelations about the widespread cheating by MPs on their expenses, Powell had a fairly jaundiced view about the people's elected representatives.

As it turned out, Bob Hale was a decent enough sort and the work was easy. A few over excited protesters and the occasional approach from a stranger on the street, didn't add up to any serious threat. The hours of work were flexible, which was another way of saying he ended up working long days. He wondered if the public understood how hard politicians worked?

Parliament was closed for the holidays but Bob still had frequent meetings in London, which sometimes went on long into the night. Bob would book them rooms at a smart hotel close to Victoria station when it became too late to return to Brighton. On more than one occasion, Bob would meet someone over dinner in a fancy restaurant and Powell would get to eat a Big Mac from a street corner outside the restaurant. The expenses account didn't stretch to Powell also enjoying fine dining.

As the month drew to an end, Powell was thinking he would miss Bob and the other members of his team. Top of the list he would miss was Hayley Carter, Bob's very attractive and efficient personal assistant. Powell had remained professional but he felt the electricity when she was near and their jobs meant they were both around Bob and thus each other a great deal of time. Powell was uncertain if she had any of the same feelings for him but he had decided he would invite her out to dinner once Bob left for his holiday in Spain. She had asked to see his bar but he would be staying well clear with Afina in her current mood.

Bob Hale lived in a large detached house in Ovingdean, a small village on the edge of Brighton. Powell collected him each morning at eight and drove him the ten minutes to his office in Kemptown, a small but bustling neighbourhood on the east of Brighton.

"I won't need you tonight Powell, after you drop me home," Bob said from the back seat of the car. "I'm going to a party at a friend's house in Haywards Heath and I can drive myself."

"I don't mind dropping you off and picking you up," Powell volunteered.

"That won't be necessary. I may well end up staying the night. You haven't had many free nights since you started working for me so go out and have some fun."

"Okay. If you're sure?"

"I shall be perfectly safe without you for one night."

"Will you be going in the office tomorrow?"

"Yes. I have a lot to tidy up before I go on holiday. If I do decide to stay over, I'll get back here early in the morning so pick me up at eight as usual."

"Will do."

"Listen, I would have liked to say thanks properly for your efforts over the last month but I'm up to my eyes in work so how about Hayley takes you out to dinner tonight at my expense?"

"That isn't necessary," Powell replied. "I've just been doing my job." He was fully aware Bob delegated as much as possible to Hayley but she was sitting next to Bob and this fell outside any assistant's duties. If it didn't, it should do. "I'm sure Hayley has better things to do with her evening than take me to dinner," Powell continued. Even as he spoke the words, he couldn't believe what he was saying.

"I insist," Bob replied. "Hayley doesn't have any plans. Actually, you would be doing me a favour because Hayley also deserves a night off."

"Bob, this is getting embarrassing," Hayley interjected. "Perhaps Powell doesn't want to have dinner with me."

"It isn't that," Powell quickly replied. "I would love to have dinner with you but only if you promise not to talk about politics."

"Then it's a date," Bob smiled.

"It's not a date," Powell added hurriedly. "It's a farewell dinner between work colleagues."

"That's what I said," Bob smiled.

CHAPTER THREE

It was the first sunny day in England since Alex had arrived four days earlier. The temperature had hit twenty five degrees and the residents of Brighton, along with a large number of visitors, had flocked to the beach and the pier. It wasn't as hot as back home but it was pleasant enough to be wearing jeans and a short sleeved t-shirt.

Alex was staying in a small hotel in the centre of the city and acted much like any other tourist, spending time becoming familiar with the city. Although the focus was on routes in and out of the city, not the famous pier or Royal Pavilion. The fastest way between two points was more interesting than a swim in the sea.

It was a first visit to England and driven by necessity not pleasure. There was an urgency to accomplish the objective but thorough preparation was still vital. That was something learned in the army after eight years of training and operations. Alex had shown an aptitude for army life and the last three years had been spent as a member of the Special Operations Battalion of the Croatian army.

Alex sat drinking a beer in the garden of a pub and thought about the hectic last ten days. What strange fortune had led to watching a television news program about the British voting to leave the European Union? Politics and army life didn't really mix so Alex rarely showed any interest in the news. Who needed to sit and hear about the suffering in the world? That was no surprise to someone who had served tours of duty in various war zones.

Alex preferred to watch an action movie where the bad guys got hunted down and killed. Real life didn't always end so well. However, the remote wasn't close to hand and so the channel remained unchanged. A small act that would lead to a life changing revelation. Alex literally jumped up from the sofa like the proverbial scalded cat, when recognising the man appointed as part of the British team negotiating with Brussels.

It was a face never to be forgotten. A recurring image in nightmares. The face had aged but the eyes were the same piercing blue. The smile was the same. It was the person Alex had for many years called simply the Beast! Now the Beast had become the operational target.

Alex had rushed to the nearest computer and discovered the Beast was a member of the British Parliament, representing a constituency on the south coast of England, close to Brighton. There were plenty of photos on the internet covering the last ten years, since when he had been in politics. It was definitely the same man.

A search of the Beast's history revealed the final evidence and confirmed Alex's brain wasn't playing tricks. Although there was nothing to prove the Beast had ever visited Croatia, he had worked for the War Crimes Tribunal so it was highly likely he had made a visit. How had such a criminal ever come to work for such an organisation? It was almost comical!

Alex had plenty of holiday available to take and immediately requested two weeks leave, which was quickly granted. There were no current operations of significance in the pipeline and the officer in charge thought it a good time to be taking holiday. You could never predict what was around the corner when all leave would be cancelled at a moment's notice. It was fortunate the British had not yet left the EU and so within a week, Alex was able to freely travel to England.

Alex had spent the last couple of days reconnoitring where the target lived and the local office, where his constituents could meet with him and seek assistance with their variety of problems. Alex had seen the notice pinned to the outside of the office door, which announced the office would be closing in two days for two weeks. The target was going on holiday to Spain.

Alex had to decide whether to act quickly or follow the target to Spain. There was really no decision to make. The future was uncertain. People were run down by buses every day and there was no more to learn. Discovering the criminal had been an act of good luck. Now was not the time to risk an act of bad luck ruining the opportunity for revenge.

The first thing Alex must do was to acquire a weapon. Despite being an expert in close combat techniques and having no doubt a desk bound politician would present no challenge, striking with a knife would require getting close to the target. The politician didn't appear to have any professional security. He wasn't important enough to merit police protection but he was always accompanied by one or two colleagues and Alex didn't want them trying to be heroes, forcing Alex to kill additional people in order to escape. The politician was the only target.

Alex had made tentative enquiries about where to obtain a weapon before leaving home. There was a man in London, who could supposedly obtain any type of weapon. Alex was due to meet him in two hours so finished the beer and headed for the train station.

CHAPTER FOUR

Alex entered the pub on Whitechapel Road and immediately registered the unwelcoming looks from the men inside as they checked out the arrival of a stranger. Although this part of the East End of London was no longer the preserve of the poor and criminals, this particular pub seemed to have been bypassed by the affluent bankers and middle classes, who now flocked to the area. There were virtually no women present and the men sat grouped around small tables drinking pints of beer. Neither the location or the décor was likely to attract anything other than locals.

Alex approached the bar and a middle aged man, who seemed less than ecstatic about the arrival of a new customer, grudgingly pulled a pint of lager.

"Is Tony here?" Alex asked.

"Don't know any Tony," the barman replied.

Alex doubted the barman would admit to knowing anyone in the pub. He wouldn't win friends or customers by talking to strangers about his regulars, who managed to look suspicious just drinking their beers.

Alex paid the barman and retreated to a table in the corner. With no one any longer paying any attention to the stranger, Alex sent Tony a text asking about his whereabouts.

Five minutes later a man entered and approached the bar. He was about thirty years old and casually but stylishly dressed. The designer stubble added to the image of someone doing well in life. He ordered a beer and spoke with the barman but Alex couldn't hear what was said. After a minute, the man walked towards Alex's table carrying his beer.

"I'm Tony," he said and sat down without waiting to be invited.

Alex skipped the introductions and came straight to the point. "I'm told you can get me what I need."

"And who told you that?"

"A friend."

"Does your friend have a name?"

"Most people do."

"Are you going to tell me his name?"

"You don't know him but he made enquiries with his friends and I was given your name."

"Look, I don't know you from Adam," Tony said, leaning closer across the table. "For all I know you could be a copper and wearing a wire."

"I assume a copper is some form of police officer?" Alex spoke good English, which had been improved by intensive lessons in the army but had mainly been practised on joint operations with other forces, when English would be the common language. However, the army didn't spend much time teaching you colloquial vocabulary.

"Where the fuck are you from?" Tony asked.

"That is not important. I am not a copper and I need a weapon in a hurry. I can pay good money but if you are not interested, I do have an alternative number to call." Alex was bluffing. There was no second option.

Tony stared at Alex for a moment before speaking. "With that accent I guess you aren't British, which means you can't be a copper. And you don't look like a terrorist. I wouldn't sell to anyone I suspect of being a terrorist. What do you need?"

"Shouldn't we go somewhere more private to discuss this matter?"

"Here is just fine. Every man in here has done time."

"Done time? What does that mean?"

"Been inside. You know been in prison."

Alex leaned a little closer. "Ideally I would like a Sig 229. You know what that is?"

"Of course I fucking know what it is. But I don't have any."

"What do you have?"

"I can get you a Glock 19."

"Then I guess the Glock will have to do. I need plenty of ammunition as well. When can I get it?"

"I need half an hour."

"Then why are you still sitting here?"

"Don't you want to know how much it will cost? Glocks don't come cheap."

"So what is the price?"

"Two thousand pounds."

"Agreed." Alex could see the look of surprise in Tony's eyes. He had expected to have to haggle over the price.

"You have the money on you?" Tony asked.

"Yes."

"Then I'll go get the merchandise. Wait here for me. I should only be about twenty minutes."

"I'll be right here when you return."

CHAPTER FIVE

Tony stepped back inside the pub and nodded at Alex to join him outside. Alex walked to the door and followed Tony outside on to the street. It was still light and Tony led the way to a modest looking saloon car.

"Sorry about the mess," Tony apologised as Alex joined him in the front of the car. "I keep it like this as otherwise it becomes a magnet for any local thief."

"Do you have the weapon?" Alex asked.

"Show me the money first."

Alex took an envelope from the inside jacket pocket. "Two thousand pounds as agreed," Alex said, opening the envelope enough for Tony to identify a wad of fifty pound notes.

Tony reached behind and took hold of a supermarket shopping bag from the backseat. He handed the bag to Alex. "I won't even charge you the five pence for the bag," he laughed.

Alex didn't get the joke, looked inside the bag and recognised the Glock. It looked in reasonable condition. There were also two boxes of ammunition in the bag. Alex passed the envelope with the money to Tony, who immediately started to count the cash.

"Don't you trust me?" Alex asked with a small smile.

"I wouldn't trust my mother where money is concerned." Tony finished counting and put the envelope in the glove compartment. "If you need anything else, you know where to come."

Alex gave a small nod of the head. Then without further word exited the car and headed towards the underground, feeling upbeat. It felt good to be armed.

The good mood only lasted a matter of seconds. After about fifty metres there was the sound of running feet approaching fast from behind. Alex instinctively anticipated the worst and turned to face the potential threat.

Two men wearing dark hoodies confronted Alex. They were holding knives in their hands. Alex could make out one man was black and the other was white. The knives appeared to be kitchen knives rather than true weapons. There was no time to reach into the plastic bag for the gun, not that it was likely to be needed. Two street fighters would have to get very lucky to have any chance against a Krav Maga expert.

"Give us your wallet and phone," the black man said, brandishing his knife menacingly. "And you can hand over the bag as well."

Alex said nothing and didn't move.

"You fucking deaf? Hand over your wallet," the man repeated.

Alex was assessing the situation. The two men seemed to be on their own. They weren't professionals. In fact, up close they were barely men. They looked like teenagers and the nervous mannerisms suggested a drug habit. Alex placed the plastic bag on the ground.

"You have two choices," Alex replied, conversationally. "You can walk away now or you can be taken away in an ambulance. It's your choice."

The second man let out a nervous laugh. "It's you who will need the ambulance."

"I'm going to count to three," Alex warned. "One…" Alex didn't count any further but stepped towards the black man and aimed a single punch to his windpipe. The man instantly dropped his knife and clutched at his throat, desperate to get air into his lungs.

His friend looked on in shock at what had happened and before he could move, Alex put one hand on his wrist and twisted it up behind his back. Again the knife fell to the ground. Alex took hold of the index finger on the hand and snapped it backwards until it broke. The man screamed but Alex didn't let go and took hold of the next finger.

"Why did you choose me?" Alex enquired calmly.

"You broke my fucking finger," the man whimpered.

Alex glanced across at the other man who was still desperately trying to breathe and too incapacitated to cause any further trouble.

"I need you to concentrate," Alex emphasised with an extra pull upwards on the arm. At the same time starting to push the finger back. "Why did you pick on me?"

"Don't," the man begged, "Please don't. He told us you were loaded. Said if we took the gun back we could keep the rest."

"Who told you?"

"Tony of course. We work for him."

"I'd find a new employer." Alex gave a last squeeze of the man's arm and pushed him in the direction of his friend before picking up the plastic bag and walking back towards the pub. A couple across the street had witnessed what took place but when Alex looked in their direction, they hurried on their way.

The car was still parked on the side of the road but there was no sign of Tony. He would no doubt be in the pub enjoying a drink and waiting for his men to return. Alex smiled. Tony was in for a surprise.

Tony was not the first opponent to underestimate the challenge presented by Alex. Size really wasn't important. A small frame and five feet seven in height may not count as very large but lightning fast reflexes and mental toughness had earned respect from army colleagues.

Alex realised it could be dangerous walking back into the pub but Tony wasn't going to get to walk away without paying for his actions. Alex definitely wasn't someone to just forgive and forget. In the doorway of the pub, Alex took the gun from the bag before entering. Tony was sat talking to a couple of other people with his back to the door. One of the men talking to Tony looked up and seeing Alex, hurriedly said something. Tony turned around slowly and his expression showed surprise.

"There was something I forgot," Alex said, pointing the gun at Tony. "I forgot to test it works properly."

At the sight of the gun, silence descended on the pub.

"Don't be silly," one of the braver customers at another table cautioned, obviously not easily intimidated by the sight of a gun. "We've all seen your face and you can't shoot all of us."

"I have no argument with the rest of you. If you don't get involved, you won't get hurt. Stand up, Tony."

Tony didn't move.

Alex approached the table and grabbed the back of Tony's collar, pulling him to his feet while sticking the gun in his back to dissuade any further argument.

"We're leaving," Alex said to the whole pub.

"Do something," Tony pleaded.

No one made any effort to interfere. Alex reckoned they would think he had brought it upon himself. Alex pulled Tony backwards toward the entrance to the pub. People inside the bar were already turning back to their drinks.

"Move your feet faster or I may change my mind and put an end to your miserable life," Alex warned.

Once through the door to the pub, Alex swung Tony around and pushed him up against the wall. The gun was pushing into Tony's stomach.

"Have you ever seen what a stomach shot does to a man?" Alex asked. "It's a very slow, painful way to die but it's what you deserve."

Tony's face had turned a terrible pale colour. He was terrified. He obviously wasn't a man of action. He employed others to do his dirty work. "Please don't," he begged. "I'll do anything you want."

"I think, given everything that's happened, it's only fair you return my money."

"Take it," Tony said with almost a sense of relief. He slowly reached inside his pocket and withdrew the familiar envelope.

Alex took the money and put it back in the same jacket pocket it had occupied a short time earlier. "Thanks. Now, if I ever see your ugly face again, I promise I will put a bullet in your stomach and watch you bleed out. Consider this a warning. Now you can go back and finish your drink."

Tony was hesitant to move at first but Alex encouraged him by pulling him away from the wall and turning him to face the entrance to the pub. Tony took a step towards the door. Alex heard his audible exhalation of breath at the realisation he was safe. Then Alex gave him a further push in the back before walking way.

CHAPTER SIX

Powell arranged to meet Hayley at his favourite Thai restaurant in Rottingdean, which was only five minutes from where Bob lived but she had never been before. They arrived in separate taxis and he stood up to greet her as she entered the restaurant. Most of the diners in the restaurant also looked in her direction.

She was completely transformed from the business woman he had been spending time with over the previous month. She was wearing leggings and a short top which revealed some seriously toned midriff. Normally she wore suits for work and her long brown hair would be scraped off her face into either a bun or a ponytail. Tonight her hair hung long and so casual you could mistake she had just got out of bed but he suspected it had taken quite a lot of effort to create the casual look, which also made her seem younger.

Her eyes had strong dark makeup and her lips were a strikingly bright red. Powell hadn't previously thought much about her age but she looked in her early thirties and she had gone up in his estimation from attractive to stunning.

The wine flowed freely and Hayley became relaxed. She seemed intent on letting her hair down in more than just the literal sense.

"Why do you spend all hours at the beck and call of Bob?" Powell asked. "I mean I like him but he's a workaholic."

"I'm ambitious. I want a career in politics and working for Bob is a fabulous opportunity."

"Have you and him ever…"

"No," Hayley quickly answered. "That would be far too complicated."

"So where's Bob gone tonight?"

"A party with his close friends. I don't get invited to them. And just as well, otherwise I'd never get anytime off."

"Does Bob have a girlfriend? I've never seen him with anyone."

"He doesn't have time for a serious relationship."

"Perhaps he will get lucky at the party."

"He better not. He can't afford a scandal," Hayley responded seriously.

"He's not a monk."

"He has to behave like one if he hopes to be Prime Minister one day. The idea of waking to find a kiss and tell story about him on the front page of the Sun is my worst nightmare."

"Does he want to be Prime Minister?"

"He wouldn't say it in public but he's very ambitious."

"And if he becomes Prime Minister, then you become what?"

"Hopefully a candidate for a safe seat."

"Wow you have everything mapped out."

Hayley smiled and raised her glass. "To the future," she toasted and touched glasses.

"The future," Powell repeated. "I've just realised I may be having dinner with the future Prime Minister of the country."

"You never know," Hayley smiled. "But enough about me. Tell me something about you. What made you become a bodyguard?"

Powell kept explanations short and changed the subject to lighter topics at the first opportunity. He had too much baggage to unload for a first date. If it even was a date.

The conversation flowed and as the waiter cleared away the plates, Powell was thinking he didn't want the evening to end.

"This has been fun," Hayley said. "It's still quite early. Let's go for a cocktail at the marina."

"Sounds good to me," Powell readily agreed.

They skipped dessert and Powell allowed Hayley to pay for the meal as it was on Bob's credit card and would be swallowed up as expenses.

They took a taxi to the marina where Hayley led the way to an American themed cocktail bar, she promised made the best cocktails in Brighton. He said he wouldn't contest the point as his bar was actually based in Hove. They both ordered a Margherita but their glasses were soon empty.

"They may be good but they aren't very big," Powell remarked, draining the last drop from his glass.

"Would you like another?" Hayley asked.

"I think I could manage another one. What about you?"

"I know a place nearby serves larger measures," Hayley smiled.

"Lead on."

Hayley led the way out of the bar and down the stairs towards the marina shops. She linked her arm in his and headed towards the nearby apartment buildings.

"Where are we going?" Powell queried. "I didn't think there were any bars in this direction."

"There aren't but I thought I'd take you back to my place. That's if you don't mind? I have plenty to drink and I will be able to kick off my shoes and relax. Heels are only bearable for so long."

"Aren't you worried about the potential for scandal?" Powell teased.

"What scandal? We're just going back to discuss tomorrow's schedule," Hayley said with a straight face.

Powell hoped she was joking. He stopped walking. Hayley was still holding on to his arm and turned to look at him with a quizzical expression. As he looked into her eyes, he gently pulled her closer. He met no resistance as their lips touched and his kiss was returned and developed further as Hayley gently probed his mouth with her tongue.

After a minute he pulled away. "I think tomorrow's schedule will have to wait."

CHAPTER SEVEN

Alex patiently waited for the familiar car to arrive. The routine was that the driver stopped to allow the target and the woman out of the car, before then going to find a parking space. That was the time to strike but where was the bloody car? They were late. Had the target decided not to visit the office because he was shortly to go to Spain? Perhaps he was at home packing for his bloody holidays? Alex couldn't spend all morning hovering in the same spot without attracting attention.

A taxi pulled to a halt and a woman stepped out, who Alex immediately recognised as part of the target's team. What the hell was going on? Alex was relieved to see others disgorge from the taxi. The woman was joined on the pavement by the target and the normal driver. Despite not being religious, Alex gave a small prayer of thanks. The target and driver stopped to wait while the woman leaned through the taxi window, paying the driver. Alex was on the other side of the road and the taxi was blocking any worthwhile view of the target.

Alex was prepared for the moment when the taxi would pull away, presenting a clear shot at the target. The taxi though was showing no urgency to move on. Alex decided to cross the road to get nearer the target. The woman had received her change. Any second the group would walk away.

There was a steady stream of traffic overtaking the parked taxi, which made it difficult to cross the road. The gun was hidden in the sports bag, which hung from Alex's right shoulder. With one hand in the bag, holding the gun and ready to fire, there was finally a gap in the traffic.

Alex walked around the back of the vehicle so as to come up

behind the target. The small group were walking towards the office. Alex accelerated pace and the target was only a few steps ahead but the girl had dropped behind him and was obstructing the view. Alex realised there was only seconds left to take the shot as they would shortly disappear inside the office.

The man walking with the target turned around to say something to the girl and their eyes met. There was instant recognition of danger in the man's eyes. Alex had underestimated the target's assistant. Something about the way Alex was approaching had made the man wary, because he immediately took a step backwards in Alex's direction, blocking the pavement.

Alex had been taught never to be indecisive on an operation. If you wavered even for a second, you gave your opponent time to strike. Alex had no shot at the target with the man in his way. He needed to be removed.

As an expert in Krav Maga, Alex didn't hesitate, aiming a kick at the man's groin and was shocked when the man easily deflected the leg away with his arm. His reactions were fast. Alex followed up with a blow to the neck but again the opponent moved quickly and stepping backwards, brought his leg up in a lightning fast kick at Alex's solar plexus, which Alex only just managed to avoid by turning sideways.

This was not going to plan. This man was well trained. He wasn't just a driver. The target had turned to see what was happening and the woman was shouting something into her phone. Alex needed to neutralise the man urgently and get to the target before it was too late. In desperation, Alex reached inside the bag and withdrew the gun.

Powell had turned to smile at Hayley. He hadn't stopped smiling since she took him back to her apartment. The lean looking, athletic figure in the hoody, who was approaching fast, immediately caught his attention. He looked out of place on the street and more like a man on a mission. Powell couldn't see much more than the eyes but they were focused straight ahead and spelt danger.

Powell avoided the first kick to his groin with ease but the way the assailant followed up with a blow to his neck signalled his intent. If the blow had landed it would have been the end of the fight. This was not just some amateur protester.

Powell lashed out with a kick to the attacker's stomach but never connected as he turned sideways to avoid the blow.

"Hayley, get Bob inside the office," Powell shouted as he prepared for a further attack. He didn't envisage this man would give up easily. Neither did he feel confident he had the superior fighting skills. He needed to buy time until Bob was safe.

The assailant was reaching into his bag and when he withdrew his hand, Powell's worst fears were realised. The man had a gun in his hand.

The attacker's hand came up and fired even as Powell was aiming a kick at the man's arm to deflect his aim. The blast of the gun assaulted Powell's ears but a split second later the gun flew out of the man's hand as Powell landed his kick.

Powell followed up with a spinning kick to the knee, hoping to disable the man but he again moved too quickly.

"Powell, Bob's been shot," Hayley screamed.

Other people in the street were screaming and scurrying away from the danger. It was a chaotic scene.

The attacker looked towards the doorway over Powell's shoulder. His weapon had been knocked into the road. He seemed to assess his options, then turned on his heels and sprinted away.

Powell had no interest in giving chase. He turned back towards Bob, who was sprawled on the ground clutching at his shoulder. Powell breathed a sigh of relief as he made the quick deduction Bob would live.

CHAPTER EIGHT

Powell stayed with Bob at the hospital just in case the attacker should try again. Hayley kept him company and they were joined by two police officers with a long list of questions.

Powell gave a description of the assailant but other than that was unable to answer any other questions about motive. Even the description wouldn't prove to be of much use. A little below average height, Caucasian, athletic, didn't add up to much help for the police. The only distinguishing feature was the bushy moustache but that could have been purchased at a joke shop. Hayley and Bob were unable to contribute anything useful to the assailant's description.

Powell told the police it didn't seem like a typical terrorist attack, which elicited a surprised look from the police officer in charge. Who was Powell to judge what was or wasn't terrorism? Powell explained how he had some experience of terrorist attacks and religious extremists rarely remained silent during an attack. This attacker had not uttered a single word. The police officer wrote down everything Powell said in his notebook.

Powell added the attacker had seriously good fighting skills. He was definitely trained to a high standard in martial arts. Another question followed from the police officer about Powell's knowledge of martial arts and he explained he had a black belt in kickboxing. More notes were added to the notebook.

Powell was certain of one thing, this wasn't some random attack. Powell was convinced the man wasn't simply deranged. He had been cool and calculating in his actions, which combined with the gun they had recovered, suggested he was most likely a professional assassin. Someone wanted Bob dead and Powell doubted it was simply a disgruntled voter.

"You were lucky," Powell suggested as he stood by Bob's bedside.

"It had nothing to do with luck. You saved my life," Bob replied.

"I played a part but we were still lucky."

"Who was he?" Hayley asked.

"Unfortunately, this is a reflection of the times in which we live," Bob replied. "There are mad men everywhere who resort to violence. It's probably someone who didn't like the way the vote went."

"I don't think he was mad," Powell interjected. "The person who hired him may be but the man who attacked you was a highly trained professional."

Bob was thoughtful for a moment before replying. "If you're right, do you think there is a chance he will try again?"

"I honestly don't know," Powell answered.

"Surely it's unlikely he would dare try again?" Hayley asked. "He'll be trying to get as far away from here as possible."

"He might," Powell tentatively agreed. "But if I'm right and he's a professional then he isn't going to get paid until he finishes the job. I think we have to assume there is at least a possibility he will try again."

"Then we should talk to the police about what protection they are going to provide," Hayley recommended.

Bob ignored Hayley's suggestion. "Powell, I need you to stay on board. At least until they catch this man."

"I'm not sure…," Powell hesitated.

"I'll double your money," Bob offered.

"It's not an issue of money," Powell replied. "I'm sure the police will take the threat seriously and provide you with around the clock protection. They might not want me getting in the way."

"But you know what he looks like," Bob stressed.

"Barely. The description I gave the police was next to useless. I could probably walk right past him on the street and not know it was him."

"Powell's right," Hayley joined in. "We should leave it to the police?"

"The police don't have Powell's special skills," Bob responded sharply. Then added, "Sorry, I didn't mean to be rude. Someone just tried to kill me and I want Powell around if he should try again. Powell is the only reason I'm still alive."

"Okay, I'll stay around for a bit longer," Powell agreed. "But this isn't a long term arrangement. I can help you find someone capable if you need someone for longer than the next week or two."

"Fair enough," Bob agreed with a big smile.

Powell reckoned Bob was used to getting his own way. In truth, Powell's decision to stay was easy once he remembered that wherever Bob went so did Hayley. He couldn't walk away and then find out later she had been harmed during a further attempt on Bob's life. What Powell still didn't understand was why the attacker hadn't simply shot him, rather than engaged in a hand to hand fight. Perhaps he had underestimated Powell's skills. Powell couldn't rely on him making the same mistake a second time.

CHAPTER NINE

Alex ran towards the seafront and grabbed a taxi, asking to be dropped at the train station. It was possible to be on a plane from Gatwick within a couple of hours. That had been the original intention but Alex had no intention of running away with the job unfinished. The authorities would eventually track down the taxi and the driver would hopefully remember the offer of a large tip to break the speed limit and drop his fare at the station. That might divert some resources away from searching in Brighton.

From the station, Alex had only a five minute walk back to the hotel. Within a matter of hours, the police could be expected to be visiting all hotels and showing a photofit image of the attacker, who shot the local Member of Parliament. The combination of the hoody and the false moustache would make it difficult for the police but Alex wasn't willing to hang around to discover if the disguise had worked.

Alex packed a few clothes in the holdall, then cleaned the room thoroughly of any trace of fingerprints. The hotel bill was paid in advance so there was no need to formally checkout. Within an hour of the failed attempt on the target, Alex had left the hotel and headed towards the shops.

Alex found a coffee shop with free Wi-Fi and sat in a quiet corner. The news feeds were carrying first reports of the attack. At this early stage, there was no worthwhile description of the attacker being circulated. There was a brief video filmed on a camera showing Alex running away but the film contained no real clues to the identity of the attacker. Witnesses described him as average height and slim but that was as good as useless.

Alex was angry. It had been a very inept attempt at justice. The

Beast was still very much alive. Alex had been so close to killing the man but failed. A man who had caused so much heartache for so many years. Alex wasn't used to failing on missions. Why had the target changed his routine on that morning? On the other days the target and the girl had been dropped off and the car sped away, leaving an easy opportunity to strike. What bad luck had caused them to take a taxi on that morning?

The man who had protected the target was dangerous. He was experienced and moved fast. Alex didn't want to harm those around the target if possible but it might be unavoidable. The man was a bodyguard and risk came with the job.

Alex was being hunted by the police for attempted murder and hoped they wouldn't be able to trace the gun back to the man who had supplied the weapon. Tony would be able to give a full description, although he wouldn't want to admit to how he came by the description. However, without a doubt, Tony would look after number one first. He would do a deal with the police if it was to his benefit. Alex had a momentary regret for not killing the worthless bastard.

Alex could not be easily identified but getting close to the target again was going to be extremely difficult. A rifle with a scope would come in very useful. Logically, they would expect the attacker to be on the run so perhaps Alex would still have the element of surprise when trying again. That was probably wishful thinking. The target would have increased security and Alex no longer had a weapon.

Would the target still go on holiday? He must currently be in hospital but they would not keep him long with a shoulder wound. He may think it a good idea to get away and recuperate. Either way it was out of Alex's control and if he did go to Spain, then Alex would follow. If he stayed in Brighton, it gave Alex more time to prepare for the next attempt. Alex would not fail a second time.

Alex had an idea and searched the laptop for options. It was easy to find a long list of suitable girls. There was an East European profile, who seemed eminently suitable so Alex called and made the arrangements.

Alex finished drinking coffee and walked to a nearby hairdresser, who fortunately had a stylist available. Alex asked for a trim and blonde highlights, which occupied the next hour.

The next stop was down a side street at a shop offering piercings. Alex chose to have a single piercing in one ear and selected a circular ring made of silver. Alex had never had much inclination for piercings before as they were not a practical option for someone regularly engaged in hand to hand combat. Alex did however have plenty of tattoos down each arm.

A further stop in the shopping centre resulted in purchasing some more suitable clothes. Alex left the shop wearing a striped pink shirt underneath a burnt orange, floral jacket and blue jeans. It wasn't Alex's usual look. Walking down the high street, it was impossible not to notice the appreciative stares from a number of men, which confirmed the shopping expedition had achieved the desired result. Alex was pleased there was no possibility of anyone from back home witnessing this transformation. It would be difficult to live it down in the army mess.

It was now lunchtime and Alex was hungry so found a small Italian restaurant, which had a menu similar to restaurants back home. There were plenty of pasta and fish dishes to choose. Alex leisurely enjoyed a meal of grilled sea bass with fresh vegetables and a beer. The food was good and for a short time, Alex was able to relax.

Over a second espresso, thoughts turned to what to do next. Perhaps Alex had been hasty in resorting to a permanent solution as a means of delivering justice. A quick death was too easy a return for his sick crimes. He should be made to suffer. To expose and ruin the man would be an even better form of retribution. That could even lead to the vile pervert committing suicide. Now that truly would be justice.

It was a good idea but not very practical, Alex was thinking while walking to the Odeon cinema. There was only a limited amount of time Alex could remain in England before needing to be back on duty. It probably would be best to end the Beast's life. That would ensure no other children would be abused. Alex was pleased to discover the new Jason Bourne film was showing. It would provide a couple of hours off the streets and afterwards with a clear head, Alex would plan the next move.

CHAPTER TEN

Alex enjoyed the film, although it bore no resemblance to real life experiences. Bourne and James Bond looked great on the cinema screen but both were equally unrealistic. Alex had no problem with the fight scenes but beautiful women simply didn't throw themselves at your feet every time you won a fight. And anyone trying to order a Martini at the local bar back home would get a very strange look and go thirsty.

Alex had written down the name of the road where the girl lived and being close to the station, it was easy to find. The road consisted of small, newly built terraced homes. The height of respectability and no doubt a prime location for commuters to live. Standing at one end of the road, Alex telephoned the girl to be told the number of the house. It was a bit like an army operation, getting to meet up with the girl. She was careful to protect details of where she lived. Alex wondered whether the neighbours knew of the business being conducted in their road.

Alex knocked on the door and was quickly admitted by someone hiding behind the door. After stepping inside, the door was quickly closed. Alex was pleased to see the girl was exactly as in her profile pictures. She was in her mid-twenties with long dark hair and a slim but curvy body. She was wearing silky black underwear and looked worth every penny Alex was paying. She had a slightly quizzical look on her face as she told Alex to follow her and led the way upstairs to a bedroom.

"So you want to stay until morning?" the girl asked, closing the bedroom door.

Alex wondered why she had felt the need to close the door? Was there someone else in the house? Did escorts always have a male friend downstairs for their safety? Alex hadn't previously given it a thought but it would make sense and was a serious cause for concern.

"Yes, please," Alex replied, handing over the eight hundred pounds. It was part of the money recovered from the gun dealer so the way Alex saw it, tonight wasn't going to cost a penny.

The girl didn't count the money. "I'll just be a moment," she said and left the bedroom.

Was the girl about to deliver the money to her male friend downstairs? Did she have a pimp?

Alex studied the bedroom. It was modern and stylish. The lights were dimmed and scented candles were placed on top of the bedside tables. Music was playing softly. It was a romantic setting for what was fundamentally an unromantic liaison. Alex had chosen well. There was no point worrying about a possible man in the house. Even if there was someone downstairs, it didn't negate the reasons for booking the girl.

Alex sat on the edge of the bed waiting for the girl to return.

She wasn't gone long and returned carrying two glasses and a bottle of white wine. "So what should I call you?" she asked, placing everything on top of a chest of drawers.

"My name is Alex. What is your name?"

"What would you like it to be?"

Alex laughed. "Well you are beautiful so why don't I call you Linda? In my language it means beautiful."

"Where are you from?"

"I am from Croatia. And you are from Romania?"

"Yes but I have lived here for a long time."

"You really are very beautiful."

"I like you," Linda announced, closing the gap between them and lightly kissing Alex on the lips. "So Alex, I am all yours until the morning. What would you like to do with me?"

"Are you hungry? I was thinking we could go out for some dinner."

"Wouldn't you like to get to know me better first?" Linda asked seductively.

"Later. Right now there is a symphony playing in my stomach and I need to eat. What type of food do you like?"

"Chinese?"

"Good choice."

"So what would you like me to wear?"

"Wear?"

"Do I wear casual jeans or put on my best dress?"

"Casual is good."

"In that case help yourself to a glass of wine and I'll be back in five minutes."

Linda returned and suggested a Chinese restaurant close to the seafront. Alex was happy to bow to Linda's local knowledge. The restaurant was a ten minute walk and on the way Alex was surprised to see two girls kissing.

"You wouldn't see that back home," Alex said.

"Nor in Romania but that is why I love Brighton. It is very liberal. Here you can be yourself without criticism."

Alex's thoughts turned to the Beast. Was that why he was so perverted? Was this country too liberal?"

Dinner went quickly as Alex found Linda to be a fun and interesting companion. Neither of them asked anything very personal. They spoke about the music they loved and places they had visited.

"Would you like another bottle of wine?" Alex asked, halfway through the main course.

"I drank most of the first bottle. Don't you like the wine?"

"I mostly drink beer."

"Then why didn't you order one?" Linda asked, confused.

"You said you wanted wine so I was happy to share what you wanted."

Linda gave Alex a surprised look. "You aren't like the typical person I see."

"What do you mean?"

"Well for a start you dress oddly. Your clothes are very bright. Are you bisexual by any chance?"

"Because I wear bright clothes?" Alex laughed.

"Are you? I am."

"No. I am not bisexual. I don't like men."

"Is it your first time paying for sex?"

"Yes."

"Are you nervous?"

"Do I seem nervous?"

"A little."

"You are very direct."

"Do you want to fuck me?"

"I guess you will find out later."

CHAPTER ELEVEN

Alex had enjoyed sleeping with Linda. She hadn't just gone through the motions. She seemed to genuinely enjoy herself or perhaps all her clients felt the same and Linda was just good at her job. Alex did feel they connected on more than just a business relationship level. It was the reason Alex had taken her to dinner before they fell into bed. Alex had the chance to get to know Linda a little first and in that respect the experience wasn't much different to a one night stand, which was the only type of sex Alex had ever known. Relationships were for other people.

It was true Alex hadn't paid for sex before, although many army colleagues regularly paid for their pleasures, especially when they were away from home. There was a time Alex wouldn't do so on principle. Lives had been destroyed by someone paying for sex. However, Alex's views had modified with age. A visit to a strip club with army mates was an excellent way to let off steam after an operation. Sex or even the payment for sex wasn't the problem. The problem was a vile man who had abused a child. That was unforgiveable and completely outside all acceptable norms of human behaviour.

Alex glanced at the clock on the wall. It was seven thirty and Linda was showing no signs of stirring. They had made love until after midnight and Linda had set the alarm for eight. She promised they would make love one more time in the morning. Actually, she had said, no one was allowed to leave in the morning without first being fucked so they left with a big smile.

Linda didn't talk about making love. Once Alex revealed a desire to be submissive, Linda took control, obviously experienced at pushing someone's boundaries. It was fortunate Alex had a high pain threshold. Linda didn't hold back biting on nipples or introducing Alex to her collection of toys, including a wooden paddle. Alex loved everything but especially the way Linda enjoyed delivering pain. Each time the pain became too much to bear and Alex cried out, Linda would look Alex in the eyes and then bite or smack even harder. Alex never complained. Pain was the most real emotion and forced you to stay in the present, forgetting the demons of the past.

Alex tried to think about the day ahead but the close proximity of Linda's body made it difficult to concentrate. She turned on her side, exposing part of her breast and Alex felt the longing returning. It didn't seem appropriate to wake Linda to hold her to her promise so it seemed a good idea to turn away.

Alex had enjoyed more than just the great sex. It had been followed by the best night's sleep in a very long time. Alex had been able to go to sleep safe in the knowledge there would be no breaking down of the front door in the middle of the night as might have happened if staying in a hotel. There had also been none of the recurring nightmares, which had plagued sleep since discovering the man responsible for so much pain. Memories that had laid dormant for a long time were resurfacing in dreams. Linda had managed to cast the demons out for at least one night.

Alex was under no illusion the nightmares would return. Losing a sibling wasn't something the memory could wash away after one night of great sex. They had been very close when they were little. The two of them against the world. After the night that changed their lives, they had become even closer. Perhaps partly out of fear of the Beast returning or because they both realised nothing was any longer sacred. Their home wasn't safe and their mother could not be trusted to protect them from evil. They could only rely on each other. Now there was only Alex and a host of painful memories.

Nineteen was far too young to die. Addicted to drugs for two years, death as a result of a heroin overdose, was determined to be intentional suicide not an accident. Alex would never know the truth. The end was actually inevitable. Alex had tried to help but all efforts were rebuffed. A once normal, innocent, young child became a liar, thief and junky, who would do just about anything to buy the drugs that would help fuel a terrible habit. Getting a heroin fix was more important than family love.

Alex felt guilty at the thought of someone so loved committing suicide all alone, seeing nothing in life to make it worth living. Alex hoped it might have been an accidental overdose. For a long time, Alex couldn't shake off the feeling of guilt, of having failed. With the passing of time and a disciplined life in the army, the pain had eased but not gone away entirely. The good memories were few and far between but the feeling of love remained.

Since that fateful day when the Beast had entered their lives, the family had been on a downward spiral. Only one person's innocence was destroyed but the whole family were never the same again. Alex had withdrawn from the family as a safe defence mechanism, not wanting to be hurt. Alex occupied a dark space that no one could penetrate. For a short time, sordid moments in the back of cars with strangers would serve as love.

In the end, the whole family suffered the results of the abuse. Alex had a recurring nightmare reliving the night when the Beast came to their house. What type of mother sold their child to a man? No amount of money was sufficient recompense to excuse what took place. Life was tough for everyone in those days but other parents didn't sell their daughters. Alex left home at seventeen to join the army and escape the madness.

Alex turned thoughts back to the present. The first job of the day would be to discover whether the Beast was still in hospital. After leaving Linda, Alex would call the hospital and find out. Hospitals were easy places to infiltrate with people always coming and going.

"Would you like a quick shower?" Linda asked, breaking Alex's chain of thought.

Alex turned towards her and smiled. "Actually, I would."

"Go ahead. I'll put some coffee on."

Alex climbed out of bed and headed to the bathroom. Linda had already provided a towel the previous evening. Alex could hear the sounds of Linda moving about downstairs in the kitchen. Thoughts of there being someone else in the house were long gone. Alex had asked on returning from the restaurant whether they were alone in the house and Linda had been happy to provide a tour of the house but Alex accepted her assurance they were indeed alone.

Alex was enjoying the hot shower when the door to the bathroom opened and without saying anything, Linda slid back the shower door and stepped inside.

"I thought I'd scrub your back," she explained.

"That's big," Alex said, staring at the large strapon around Linda's waist.

"It gets to the places others don't reach," Linda laughed.

Alex was pleased to have the opportunity to enjoy Linda further. In fact, Alex couldn't think of a better way to start the day. It was already beyond the time Alex had paid for but Linda didn't seem to be clockwatching. Linda deserved every penny she earned. Few people were as enthusiastic in their work as Linda.

Linda kissed Alex on the lips, who didn't need a second invitation, passionately returning the kiss. Linda then moved down to Alex's nipples, which were sensitive from the previous night. Linda licked and bit gently on each in turn, knowing they couldn't take the type of punishment she had provided last night. After a moment, she slid to her knees and buried her face between Alex's legs.

The water cascaded off her head as she licked and sucked. Her hands were gripping Alex's buttocks. Alex in turn was gripping Linda's hair encouraging her to continue, not that she was showing any inclination to stop. Alex played with Linda's nipples and moaned in pleasure.

Linda smiled up at Alex and suddenly climbed to her feet. "Turn around," she instructed. "Open your legs and stick your bottom out."

Alex did as instructed and prepared to receive Linda's toy.

"I had a fun time last night," she said, conversationally. "But I couldn't let you leave without this experience." Linda pushed the toy a little way into Alex's bottom.

"I had fun last night," Alex agreed.

"What about now?" Linda asked and thrust the toy hard inside to its maximum length.

"Thank you," Alex replied.

Linda repeated several deep strokes and then reached her hand around and between Alex's legs to encourage a climax.

It took only a minute for Alex to experience a mind blowing orgasm.

Linda withdrew the toy and kissed Alex on the neck. "You really are fun to play with. "

Alex turned back around and kissed Linda lightly on the lips. "So are you. That was an amazing way to start the day."

Linda smiled broadly. "I always take particular care of my overnight guests. If you come back to England, I hope you will come and see me again."

"That's guaranteed."

"Good. I will go make some coffee. Take your time." Linda pulled back the shower door and left Alex to finish showering.

When Alex left the house twenty minutes later, it was with a very large smile.

CHAPTER TWELVE

Powell and Hayley collected Bob from the hospital almost exactly twenty four hours after he had been shot. Getting a bullet in the shoulder didn't qualify as serious enough to warrant keeping a bed any longer. Powell understood the NHS was under pressure but he was still surprised Bob was being released so quickly.

"Are the police making any progress?" Bob enquired, once they were all back at his house.

"If they are, they aren't saying," Powell replied.

"I thought they were going to provide protection?" Hayley queried.

"There's a policeman parked outside," Powell answered.

"One man?" Hayley asked incredulously. "That isn't enough. Bob, you know the Chief Constable. You need to speak with him and get more men. They aren't taking this very seriously."

"Cutbacks I'm afraid," Bob explained. "It's what I expected and I can't expect preferential treatment. That's why I was so keen to keep Powell."

"I'm going to start doing my job and take a look around the house, if you don't mind?" Powell questioned. Although Powell had been inside the front door many times, he'd never actually been shown around the house in its entirety.

"Hayley can show you around," Bob suggested. "I'm going to catch up on the news on my computer."

Hayley provided the guided tour of the house. Powell was slightly surprised she was so well acquainted with the upstairs rooms in the house but said nothing. They had enjoyed a great night together but events had overshadowed everything since and he had at least temporarily put his feelings for Hayley on the back burner.

There was no sign of Bob when they returned to the living room.

"I'll make some tea," Hayley volunteered and headed to the kitchen.

Bob entered the room a minute later, returning his phone to his pocket. "I'm going out this evening," he announced.

"I'm not sure that's such a good idea," Powell cautioned.

"A friend of mine just suggested an impromptu party to celebrate my good luck," Bob explained. "Just a couple of good friends and a few drinks." Seeing Powell's disapproving look he added, "I refuse to lock myself away in this house, afraid to venture out."

"I'm sure I remember hearing the doctor say you shouldn't be mixing alcohol with the pills you've been given."

"Nonsense. He just said it would make me drowsy and I shouldn't drive, which I'm obviously not going to do with my arm in a bloody sling."

"I'm coming with you," Powell stated firmly.

"Of course. You can drive me."

Hayley entered with three mugs of tea. "Where are we going?" she asked.

"Powell is taking me to my friend's in Haywards Heath tonight."

"Should you…"

"Not you as well, Hayley," Bob interrupted. "I'm going. I've given up on my holiday and need to relax."

Hayley looked at Powell and shrugged.

"I've promised to be on my best behaviour," Bob added.

"I'll let the policeman know our plans," Powell said.

"Must we take him in tow everywhere we go?" Bob asked.

"Yes is the short answer," Powell confirmed. He thought it a strange comment from Bob. He'd been desperate to get police protection.

"Do you want me to come?" Hayley asked.

"Take the night off," Bob replied. "This is a boys night out."

CHAPTER THIRTEEN

Alex had telephoned the hospital, pretending to want to visit the patient and discovered the Beast had already been released. Alex deposited the holdall at the left luggage office at the station and then walked into town, intent on getting some breakfast. A night with Linda left you ravenous.

After a large breakfast, Alex found an expensive cook shop selling high quality chef's knives. There was a fantastic selection of sharp knives, which were fit for purpose. Alex balanced a few in each hand until finding the perfect combination of balance and power. Alex decided on a set of three knives of Oriental design, which cost four hundred pounds in total. A ridiculous amount to pay for the purpose for which they were designed but cheap for Alex's purpose. One knife should be sufficient but this time Alex was preparing for the unexpected.

The second shop Alex visited provided everything needed to dress and look like a clown. It was the perfect disguise and especially as there was a current craze for people dressing as clowns and running around town scaring people. Alex chose a costume with a mask, not wanting to mess around with makeup. The mask had a white face with a red nose and a mop of long red hair.

Alex then walked to a flower shop on Western Road and purchased a huge bouquet of brightly coloured flowers. Satisfied with the shopping, Alex went for a coffee and used the disabled toilet to change clothes. There were a few strange looks as Alex emerged from the toilet as a clown but no one said anything.

Alex crossed the road and hurried towards the busy shopping centre car park, receiving amused looks from everyone on the way. Alex headed directly to the ground floor of the multi storey car park, wanting to be as close to the exit as possible. Alex identified a middle aged woman paying her parking ticket at the machine and followed her back to her car, which happened to be a Kia. Alex waited for the woman to unlock the car and then pounced on her as she was about to take her seat. Alex grabbed the woman's wrist and easily freed both the keys and car park ticket from her grip.

The woman screamed but Alex twisted her arm a little and pushed her out of the way. Without hesitation, Alex jumped in the car and drove the short distance to the exit. In the rear mirror, the woman could be seen shouting and pointing at her car. Alex would have preferred to steal a car without scaring the woman and Jason Bourne would have hotwired a car but in reality, modern technology in cars made that almost impossible. At the exit barrier it wasn't even necessary to put the ticket in the machine as sensors read the number plate and up went the barrier of its own accord.

Alex didn't normally advocate a frontal assault but this was not a typical operation. The best chance of success was to strike quickly. Even so, Alex was careful to keep within the speed limit along the sea front, not wishing to be stopped by the local police. Alex knew it would take twelve minutes to reach the target's house in Ovingdean.

Alex parked the car a short distance away from the large house. It was a quiet road full of imposing properties. The sort of homes that Alex could never hope to own. The Beast didn't deserve to own such a large house. Alex strode purposefully towards the gated entrance, holding the flowers out in front and keeping an eye out for the inevitable police presence.

Alex was almost at the entrance when spotting the lone figure sitting in the car. It didn't look as if the police were taking the threat of a second attack very seriously. The police officer quickly stepped out of his car as he saw Alex approaching.

"Can I help you?" the policeman asked formally. "I'm a police officer." He held up his badge to prove the point.

"Actually, I do like men in uniforms," Alex replied, fluttering eyelashes. "I'm delivering flowers to number sixteen." It was a difficult act to play but necessary.

"Why are you dressed as a clown?"

"People pay extra for me to deliver the flowers dressed as a clown. I guess they think it adds to the fun."

"I'll take the flowers for you," the policeman offered, holding out his arms.

"That would be very sweet of you but I'm supposed to deliver them to the front door. I'm sure you're a very nice man but how do I know you won't keep them for yourself?"

"Okay. I'll walk with you to the front door."

"What a lovely idea. And if you want, I can leave you my phone number. Just in case you should ever want me to deliver you some flowers."

"My WIFE likes flowers," the policeman emphasised. "I'm not so keen."

"Suit yourself. You're obviously very repressed."

"I am not repressed. Follow me," the policeman instructed, intent on bringing the conversation to an end and heading for the front door.

Alex followed for a couple of paces, then dropped the flowers on the ground and at the same time sprung forward and chopped to the side of the policeman's exposed neck. Alex measured the power of the blow so as not to be fatal but the policeman still collapsed towards the ground. Alex caught him on the way down and pulled the man's body behind a tree. He would only be out cold for a few minutes so it was necessary to act fast. Alex tied the man's wrists and ankles with plastic ties.

Next, Alex felt beneath the man's jacket and was excited to find a firearm. Alex had hoped that if they assigned protection it would be an armed police officer. Alex removed the gun from its holster and then picked up the flowers. They were the excuse for knocking on the front door and would hide the gun.

Alex hoped no one had been watching from the house and walked directly to the front door. There was a door bell, which Alex rang and could hear chime within the house. Then there was the sound of footsteps.

A woman opened the door, who Alex recognised as the assistant. Her face lit up when she saw the large bunch of flowers.

Alex hit her square on the jaw but only with half force, which was still enough to send her spinning back into the house and collapse on the floor.

"Who is at the door?" a male voice enquired from within the house.

Alex stepped over the body of the woman and advanced towards the sound of the voice.

CHAPTER FOURTEEN

Powell heard the ring of the doorbell and assumed it was the police officer wanting to use the bathroom again. Either that or he wanted another cup of tea. Powell was of the opinion, the calibre of officer assigned suggested the police considered the odds of another attack virtually zero.

"I'll go," Hayley announced from the hallway before Powell could move.

Powell heard the front door being opened and then a sound which didn't sound right, rather like something heavy falling to the ground.

"Who is at the door?" he shouted out, concerned and rising from his seat in the living room.

As the clown figure appeared in the doorway brandishing a gun, Powell had a sickening feeling in the pit of his stomach.

"On the floor," the clown commanded. His English was clear but there was the definite trace of an accent.

Powell calculated his chances of disarming the man but didn't like the odds. There was too much distance between them. He had to assume, despite the difference in appearance, it was the same man from the previous day. The clown was the same build.

"He's not here," Powell tried to bluff.

"If you are not on the floor in three seconds, I will shoot you."

Powell didn't believe it was an idle threat and didn't fancy being shot for the second time in less than a year. He lay face down on the carpet. He turned his head sideways to observe what the man was doing.

"Hands behind your back," the clown ordered.

Powell did as instructed and felt his hands being secured by ties. Shortly afterwards his feet were also tightly secured.

The man didn't waste time and hurriedly left the room. As soon as he was gone, Powell first moved to a kneeling position and then stood up. He jumped forwards in small steps until he reached the hallway. He could see Hayley on the floor but ignored her and headed to the kitchen.

He could hear the man moving around upstairs. A wooden block on the worktop contained a set of knives. He jumped backwards on to the worktop and shuffled further backwards until his hands were close to the knives. He slid one out of its resting place, hoping it would be sharp.

He managed to slice the plastic tie without giving himself more than a small cut in his wrist. Within seconds he had also cut the binds around his ankles. He kept hold of the knife as he returned to the hall.

Hayley was stirring, which was a good sign. Powell helped prop her against the wall. He took his phone from his pocket and called the emergency services. He passed the phone to Hayley.

"Tell them what's happened," he instructed. "The man is still in the house and he is armed."

Powell didn't understand why he hadn't heard any shots from upstairs. He didn't see how he could race up the stairs to confront the man, armed with just a kitchen knife but neither could he do nothing.

Powell cautiously climbed the stairs. He could hear movement in the end bedroom, which belonged to Bob. As he reached the top of the stairs, the assassin emerged from bob's bedroom at the other end of the landing.

"Where is he?" the clown shouted.

"He went out," Powell lied.

"Fuck! He has nine lives. Get back down the stairs. I'm leaving."

Powell backed slowly down the stairs. He had a feeling this man didn't want to shoot him but an even stronger feeling the man wouldn't hesitate to shoot if it was necessary for him to escape.

"Hurry up." The man shot at the wall beside Powell and he

accelerated his pace.

In the Hallway, Powell moved well away from the door and watched as the man ran out. Powell had no intention of giving chase and pushing his luck any further.

"Are you alright?" he asked, turning back to Hayley.

"I'll live. What about Bob?"

"He seems to have disappeared."

CHAPTER FIFTEEN

The police arrived at the house in numbers that disproved there was any manpower shortage. Powell wondered if they were trying to get in the Guinness book of world records. Two ambulances arrived, which took Hayley and the police officer to hospital, although both protested they were okay.

Powell had looked at Hayley's head and checked her jaw wasn't broken. She had a cut on the back of her head where she hit the floor, which was going to leave her with a nasty headache but otherwise she seemed okay. There were no signs of concussion but head injuries always required a visit to hospital for a proper check-up.

The policeman in charge, who had introduced himself as Chief Inspector Bailey, was asking Powell to explain what had happened when Powell's phone rang.

"Where are you, Bob?" Powell asked.

"I'm about a ten minute walk from the house. I happened to be looking out of the window when I saw a clown carrying flowers attack the police protection officer. When he entered the house, I went out of the bedroom window. I used to take the same route as a kid."

Thanks for warning the rest of us, Powell thought but said nothing. "It's safe to come back," he confirmed. "The police are here."

Powell ended the call and explained to the Chief Inspector about Bob's escape from the house.

"So this man was dressed as a bloody clown?" Chief Inspector Bailey asked in a weary voice.

"Afraid so," Powell replied. "I can tell you the clown was approximately the same height and build as yesterday's attacker but other than that…" Powell was unable to add anything useful to the description he had provided the previous day.

"Do you mind coming down the station and giving us a detailed statement? I'll have someone give you a lift and drop you wherever you want after," the Chief Inspector requested pleasantly.

"Of course. Are you going to leave some extra bodies here to protect Bob?"

"I'll see what we can do. In the short term there will be a team here combing the house for clues. Longer term, I'll speak to my boss."

"Good."

"Do you think he's going to try again?"

"I get the feeling he's not going to give up. I hope I'm wrong."

It was a couple of hours before Powell returned to Bob's house. A police car dropped him off and the gardens and house were still swarming with police. Some were scouring everywhere for clues to the identity of the attacker. Others looked as if they were there purely for protection as they patrolled the grounds.

Bob was sat in the living room with what looked like a glass of whisky in his hand.

"Can I get you a drink," Bob offered. "I bloody needed one after all that."

"I'm fine thanks. How is Hayley?"

"She went to the hospital."

"I know but how is she doing?"

"I haven't heard."

Powell took out his phone and called Hayley's number.

"Hello," she answered.

"What do the doctors say?"

"I have to spend the night here. When I fell back, I landed on my head and they want to keep an eye on me in case of concussion."

Powell smiled at the other end of the phone. Hayley didn't seem to remember him checking her head wound. Concussion may have been delayed but seemed a distinct possibility.

"I actually feel okay," Hayley continued. "They gave me some strong pain killers and to be honest I can't feel a thing."

"A night in hospital sounds a good idea. In fact, you may want to reconsider whether you come back to work at all until this man is caught. It's dangerous spending time around Bob."

"But then I wouldn't get to spend time with you," Hayley replied, a little tongue in cheek.

"I can fully understand why you would find it difficult to keep your hands off me but it is only temporary."

"Hopefully they will catch him before tomorrow."

"They are going to broadcast an appeal for information all over the local news tonight so I doubt he will stay around here very long." Powell wasn't entirely convinced by his own argument. He had a nagging fear this man simply wouldn't give up until he had succeeded in killing Bob. It seemed almost personal. What had Bob done to this man?

CHAPTER SIXTEEN

Powell had argued at first against the idea of Bob visiting his friend but not for nothing was Bob known as an excellent debater in the House of Commons. Bob sounded a bit like Churchill as he spoke of refusing to be cowed by the threat of attack. He was not going to be intimidated into raising the drawbridge and staying at home, like a hermit.

Powell was amused by the rhetoric but there was some logic to Bob's argument. Even the presence of armed police protection could not guarantee his safety at home. After all, the attacker knew where he lived and had already demonstrated he was willing to risk an attack on the home. It might actually be a good thing to get out of Brighton.

The police were not keen on the idea of Bob leaving the house but being a Member of Parliament, with friends in high places, carried enough clout for Bob to get his way. The police could hardly lock him inside his own home. It was ultimately his decision and they soon realised, he wasn't going to be dissuaded from going out.

The drive to Haywards Heath took twenty five minutes. Powell pulled up in front of the large iron gates, which sat in the midst of a high, brick wall circling for as far as he could see in each direction down the road. He could see a glimpse of an impressive home hidden behind the gates. Bob obviously had wealthy friends.

Powell opened his car window and started to speak into the entry phone system. Before he had announced who was visiting, the gates swung open and a mini shot through the gates, kicking up the small pebbles that covered the drive as he accelerated too fast and his tyres tried to find grip. Powell glared at the driver who ignored him and revved his engine even more before pulling onto the road.

Powell returned to the entry phone and announced their arrival.

The gates were halfway shut but quickly swung back open again. He hadn't bothered to ask the name of the friend they were visiting. It didn't seem relevant but he had assumed it would be someone wealthy but of little real interest. He was quite taken aback when the front door of the large country house was opened by Jack Street, who qualified as a national institution. For some reason, Powell had never considered Bob interesting enough to have showbiz friends let alone such a famous singer. A rather harsh thought he realised as soon as it crossed his mind.

The two police officers remained in their car on the driveway, declining the offer to venture inside the house. They were responsible for external security and Powell would stay close to Bob inside the house. Powell was very happy with the arrangement. He was entirely confident it would be a quiet evening. He was shown to the kitchen where he was introduced to the housekeeper.

Sara May looked as if she enjoyed eating her food as much as she professed to enjoy cooking. She looked a formidable woman and the kitchen was her domain.

"Take a seat," she instructed. "I've made you some ham and gherkin sandwiches on rye bread. I'll make some tea."

Powell was peckish and about to eat when he remembered his manners. "Are you going to be joining me for a sandwich?" he asked.

"I've eaten, thanks. You go ahead and start eating."

"These are good sandwiches," Powell commented after a few mouthfuls. "Do you cook all Jack's meals?"

"I do cook for Mr. Street," Sara confirmed. "He likes my food," she added proudly.

"I'm sure he does. How long have you worked for Jack?"

"I've been working for Mr. Street for getting on twenty years," Sara replied.

After such a long time working for him, Powell thought she might have at least called him by his first name. Perhaps they did in private and it was just Powell's presence making her formal.

"That's a long time."

"How long have you worked for Mr. Hale?"

"Only a few weeks."

"And what is it exactly you do for him?"

"I'm his bodyguard." Powell didn't like the description but it was the reality and the simplest explanation of his role.

"Really. You don't look mean enough to be a bodyguard."

"Well I'm definitely not mean by nature but that is my current job. To be honest, I own a bar in Brighton and that occupies most of my time. I'm helping Bob out as a favour to a friend."

"Mr. Street has security. They do look mean. He gave them the night off tonight."

"Well we shouldn't need them. We have two armed police officers outside."

"Mr. Street always gives them the night off when Mr. Hale and his other friends visit."

"Is he good friends with Bob?"

"Mr. Hale is a regular visitor."

"How did they meet?"

"I'm not sure. As you can imagine, Mr. Street meets a huge number of people."

Powell found Sara quite guarded in her responses. "I bet you know all Jack's secrets," Powell probed. "You could probably make a fortune if you ever sold your story to the newspapers."

Sara pushed back her chair and stood up. "I would never dream of cashing in on my position in that way. Mr. Street is a wonderful employer and a wonderful man."

"I'm sure he is," Powell quickly agreed. "I didn't mean to infer you would take advantage of your position. It's good to meet someone who is loyal and hardworking."

Sara sat back down. "I am very loyal to Mr. Street," she stressed. "He treats me well and does a great deal for charity you know?"

"I didn't know but that's good to hear."

Powell was a sceptic about most things in life but was pleased to hear Jack Street really was one of the good guys. He had an unsullied reputation after spending over forty years in the music industry, not something many musicians could claim.

Bob and Jack Street were sipping expensive brandy in the living room.

"This isn't exactly what I planned for tonight," Jack apologised.

"Can't be helped," Bob replied. "I'm sure everything will go back to normal once they catch this madman."

"Do the police have any idea who he is?"

"Not a clue."

"I have someone special lined up for when you get rid of your police entourage."

Bob's ears pricked up. "How special?"

"Very special. I've met her a couple of times and she really is the cutest little thing ever."

"Have you yet sampled her delights?"

"No. I thought I'd give you the first opportunity."

"You must need a very big favour," Bob smiled.

"It's the least I can do for you after all you've been through recently."

"And what's the favour you need?" Bob repeated, smiling.

"Am I that transparent? Remember that party a few months back where I met a couple of your political friends?"

"I do indeed. It was quite a night."

"Well, I'd like you to invite Ed Manners to your place and invite me over as well"

"Who is supplying the entertainment?"

"I can provide everything needed for a great evening."

"Including that special girl you mentioned?"

"Yes including her."

"Will she be open to playing with me even if you are there?"

"I don't think that will be a problem."

"You know Ed prefers boys?"

"So do I sometimes. I will be sure to see his needs are covered."

"I don't know how you always manage to find exactly the right types to make us all happy."

"Youngsters are always drawn to money and fame. I have both and I understand what they want. Most of them are completely disconnected from their parents. They want someone to make them feel special."

"What do you want from Ed?"

"I need some help with a problem."

"You know what he does for a living?"

"Yes. He works for the Home Office."

"That's only broadly true."

"What do you mean?"

"He's a big shot in the Security Services."

"I did wonder if that was the case. He hinted as much."

"And is that why you want me to organise this dinner."

"As I said, he may be able to help with a problem."

"Care to share the nature of the problem?"

"Not really, Bob. It's probably best you aren't involved."

"Why don't you just invite him over here for dinner?"

"I only met him that once and he'd had a few drinks. I thought a more subtle approach might be best."

"Okay," Bob agreed. "I'll check when he's free and let you know."

"Thanks. The sooner the better."

CHAPTER SEVENTEEN

Alex had escaped in the stolen car and driven the five minute journey to the Marina. By the time the police got their act together, Alex had left the car in the free car park. The woman would eventually get her car back in one piece. Alex wasted no time in changing appearance. The loose fitting clown outfit was quickly removed, revealing jeans and a t-shirt. Alex stuffed the outfit into a shopping bag discovered in the boot of the car.

Alex exited the car and walked to the nearby taxi rank, throwing the bag of clothes into a bin outside the bowling alley on the way. Ten minutes later the taxi was in the centre of Brighton and Alex was lost in the crowds. Not that there was any desperate need to hide, just keep a low profile. The police would have an impossible task in their hunt for a clown.

More shopping was necessary. Alex purchased a smart grey suit and some low strength reading glasses. Next was a dark brown hair colour in a bottle, which promised to only take five minutes to work. Despite the police having very little in the way of a description, Alex was very aware Brighton was covered with CCTV cameras and changing appearance was a worthwhile precaution.

The magic of google and a quick call to the Prince Regent swimming pool confirmed they had individual showers available. Within an hour Alex was transformed into a business executive looking nothing like the clown, who had carried out the attack. Alex was happy with the new image.

Alex telephoned a Hilton hotel in central London to reserve a room and took the train from Brighton, collecting the holdall from left luggage. Alex looked like any other person staying at the hotel for business when checking in. It had crossed Alex's mind to pay another visit to Linda but it wasn't a good idea. She was too much of a distraction. Brighton would be flooded with police and a stay in London made more sense. It was only an hour away from the coast.

Alex had a whisky from the mini bar in the room and decided on the next move. There would be little chance to get close to the target. Alex had blown that opportunity but resolved that it would be a case of third time lucky. On the positive side, the beast was a public figure and couldn't stay hidden away for long. Next time the outcome would be different.

It was seven when Alex arrived at the pub, more in hope than expectation. It would be difficult for anyone from the first visit to recognise the new look. Anyway, they wouldn't get the chance of more than a cursory glance. Alex thought the odds were about evens that Tony would be inside the pub.

Alex entered the main bar and a quick glance revealed this was his lucky day. Tony was sitting talking to two other people. Alex paid him no particular attention. Several people checked out the new arrival in the bar but Alex avoided their stares. They went back to their drinks and Alex retreated outside as if one look was enough to decide it was the wrong place to get a drink.

Alex walked up the street a short distance until recognising Tony's car, took out a knife and sliced into one of the front tyres before doing the same to one of the rear tyres. Tony wouldn't be driving anywhere in a hurry.

Alex realised it could be a long wait until Tony left the pub so decided there was nothing to be lost by a friendly approach. Alex sent Tony a text message.

I need to make a further purchase. Can we meet at the same pub as before in about half an hour?

The reply was almost immediate.

I've never sold you anything because you never paid me.

Alex typed a response.

If you remember, that was your fault not mine. I'm on my way to the pub. I'll be there in thirty.

Alex wondered if Tony was driven more by greed or fear. It took only a minute to wait for the answer. Tony emerged from the pub and stood on the pavement looking up and down the road. Then he started to walk away from the pub towards where he had left his car. He obviously wasn't hanging around for a further encounter with Alex and risking not getting paid a second time.

Alex was hiding in a doorway close to Tony's car and stepped out from the darkness as Tony came near.

"Not very friendly of you to rush off," Alex said.

Tony jumped out of his skin. "Fuck!" He swore and looked around as if seeking help before regaining his composure. "I'm not your friend."

Alex let Tony see the large knife in his hand. "I want to do some business with you."

There was a scared look on Tony's face. "People who want to do business with me don't arrive with large knives."

"That's just a precaution. We didn't exactly part on the best of terms last time."

"You ripped me off," Tony accused.

"On the positive side, I didn't kill you. Many would have in my position."

"I'm not talking to you while you wave that knife in my face." Tony seemed to have found some backbone.

"Sorry, I wasn't trying to threaten you." Alex put the knife away. "I need a new weapon and I have cash."

Tony thought about the idea for a second. "Okay, let's get in the car," he said. As he opened the car door he noticed the flat front tyre for the first time. "Fuck, what's happened to my tyre?" It was rhetorical but then it dawned on him who was responsible. "Did you do this?"

"Sorry about that. I will pay for new tyres."

"What did I ever do to deserve meeting you?"

Tony sat in the driver's seat and Alex walked around the car to sit in the front passenger seat.

"What do you need?" Tony asked.

"An L115A3 would be perfect."

"What the fuck is that?"

"It's the long range weapon used by army snipers. Can you get one?"

"There isn't much demand for snipers around here."

"I don't need your sarcasm. I need a good long range rifle."

"I can get most things if you have enough money but it may take a bit of time to get you a fancy sniper rifle. However, I know I can lay my hands on an M16 immediately."

Alex preferred the specialist sniper weapon but time was in short supply. The American M16 would have to suffice.

"Okay, I will take the M16. How much?"

"Two thousand pounds."

"That's about twice the going rate. I'll give you one thousand pounds plus five hundred for a new handgun."

Tony considered the offer.

"I'm not negotiating with you," Alex prompted. "That is a fair price. When can you get me the weapons?"

"Twenty four hours. See me here same time tomorrow."

"I'll give you five hundred in advance as a show of trust. Make sure you are here tomorrow with my weapons. If I have to come looking for you, I will not be so forgiving a second time."

CHAPTER EIGHTEEN

Powell had spent a quiet twenty four hours by recent standards. There had been no further attempts on Bob's life. Powell had spent most of the day in Hayley's company, who had returned from the hospital insisting she needed to be with Bob and ignoring Powell's advice to stay away, until it was safe to return. Bob locked himself in his study, no doubt working on matters of great importance while Powell checked and rechecked the house and grounds were secure.

As the day progressed, he found himself watching Hayley as she moved around the house. His mind was also conjuring up images of the night they had spent together, which he wanted to suppress until Bob's attacker was caught. Unfortunately that was easier said than done. Even the most innocent movement on Hayley's part was inducing a physical response he couldn't control.

Powell joined Hayley to watch the evening news and was shocked when the first item was all about Jack Street. He had been interviewed by the police in connection with the national investigation into child sex abuse.

"It's a disgrace," Haley said.

"You don't know he's guilty of anything," Powell replied.

"That's not what I mean. It's a disgrace the way they ruin his reputation by putting this all over the news. They even mentioned he's never been married. What the hell has that got to do with anything!"

"The police must have some reason to want to interview him."

"It's probably just some youngster jumping on the bandwagon."

"It's not a bandwagon if there has been actual abuse."

"This is Jack Street we are talking about. I don't believe he is guilty of child abuse. Do you?"

"Well it does seem unlikely but in my experience even the most unlikely things are possible."

"I'd better go speak to Bob," Hayley said. "See what he knows."

Powell watched the remainder of the news and then Hayley returned.

"What did you find out?" Powell asked.

"Bob says it's a load of rubbish. He says with all the focus on the lawyers resigning from the child sex abuse inquiry and what it's costing, he thinks it's an attempt to justify continuing by implicating another high profile celebrity."

Powell didn't want to argue with his employer so said nothing even though he doubted the validity of Bob's argument.

"I guess we won't be visiting Jack again in the near future."

"Well that is half true but he's coming here for dinner in a couple of days."

"Really. I didn't think a politician would want to be seen mixing with Jack while he is under investigation."

"I said something similar to Bob but he just replied Jack is innocent until proven guilty."

A nice sentiment Powell thought but not one shared by certain elements of the press.

Alex was happy to have acquired the M16 rifle and a new Glock. Tony had delivered the weapons as agreed to a slightly apprehensive Alex, who had been concerned Tony may turn up mob handed looking for revenge. In the event, it had been a simple exchange. Alex had hired a car and driven to the meeting before placing the weapons in the boot of the hired Ford Focus.

Alex would have liked to try out the M16 to check it had no idiosyncrasies but didn't know the local area well enough to identify a safe location. Alex had used the M16 many times in the past so was at least generally familiar with the weapon. As long as it wasn't a complete dud it would do the job and Tony wouldn't risk the repercussions of selling Alex anything that didn't work properly.

Alex had decided to request extended leave from the army so as not to be forced into acting before fully prepared. Fortunately, it had been quickly approved. Alex had been given a further week, which should be sufficient time to achieve the objective. There was no guarantee it would be enough time but Alex had no intention of not returning to the army on time so needed to act fast. It would then be necessary to get out of the UK as quickly as possible. And it would probably be many years before a return visit.

Alex was in a quandary. The target could stay holed up in the house for the next week and time was at a premium. At the most, Alex knew there would only be time for one more attempt. Where the man lived was a fundamental problem because Alex couldn't easily watch the house during the day. The house was in the middle of a suburban street full of expensive homes. The police were on high alert and would no doubt be highly suspicious of anyone they found in close proximity of the house without a valid reason. Even armed with a rifle, it was difficult to get near enough with any realistic chance of success. There were no vantage points overlooking the house.

The Beast had planned to be on holiday in Spain so there would be no public engagements currently organised in the UK. However, it was probably safe to assume he would have a full diary from when he was due to return, which was only another three days away. Alex's research had also revealed the English Parliament would reopen in exactly one week's time. It was reasonable to assume all Members of Parliament would attend the opening and that would involve travelling to London, which would create opportunities to strike.

Alex could think of no way of drawing the target out of his house. A night time assault on the house was a possibility but the last twenty four hours had given time for reflection. Alex was hiding in plain sight by staying at a quality hotel in central London, posing as a business executive. Alex needed to face up to the reality of the situation. If Alex could not come up with a plan within the remaining ten days of holiday, then it may be necessary to exercise caution and think about going home, returning at some point in the near future. Although Alex wanted the man dead, this was not a suicide mission. Alex would not become another of the Beast's victims.

Alex had been consumed by a strong desire for revenge and started to behave recklessly, which went against all the years of training. Alex had waited too many years to gain revenge for what the man had done to the family. It would be stupid and senseless to now mess things up for the sake of a few more months. There would be no point in getting caught and rotting in jail while the target was still walking the streets.

CHAPTER NINETEEN

Powell was told he wasn't needed for the visit of Jack Street. Bob insisted he should take Hayley out to dinner and he didn't want to see either of them again until the morning. Bob obstinately refused to listen to Powell's protests and dire warnings. He pointed out the two armed police officers were still parked in the driveway and they offered sufficient protection. Powell didn't entirely agree but he had been cooped up in the house for so long he was excited by the chance to get out, particularly as it involved taking Hayley to dinner.

Despite Hayley wanting to visit his bar, he pointed out he viewed his bar as his workplace and it was not somewhere he went to relax and have fun. They settled on taking a taxi into the centre of Brighton. Powell introduced Hayley to a small cocktail bar above the Theatre Royal and after two Margaritas each, they walked to a nearby Thai restaurant.

"Do you think Bob's safe now?" Hayley asked.

"You mean tonight or generally?"

"Generally. There have been no more attacks for a few days. Do you think the danger is over?"

Powell didn't rush to answer. "To be honest, I don't know. Someone seemed very intent on murdering Bob. Whatever his motivation, there's no reason to think his motivation has lessened by having failed twice."

"So you think he'll try again?"

"Let's put it like this, I don't think we should relax until they catch the man responsible for the previous attacks."

Hayley drank some of her wine. "I can't believe how my life has changed since we last went out to dinner. Bob was going to Spain. My career was on track and my private life was on the up."

Powell gave a reassuring smile. "Isn't your career still on track?"

"Not if Bob gets himself killed. He also could be tainted by his obstinate refusal to stay away from Jack Street. The Prime Minister won't be around for long and Bob has a strong chance to be the next leader if he keeps his reputation clean."

"Is he that popular with his colleagues?"

"Let's say he has less enemies than most."

"Not exactly a ringing endorsement of his qualities."

"He's a good man but that isn't enough to get elected leader. You need support from both sides of the party. He is the best compromise candidate."

"Doesn't exactly fill me with excitement that our Prime Minister is elected on the basis he is the least offensive candidate."

"You're twisting my words."

"Let's change subject," Powell suggested, seeking to avoid an argument.

"That might be a good idea," Hayley agreed with a smile.

"So what about your private life? Is that still on the up?"

"Could be," Hayley smiled. "If the damned fool doesn't get himself killed."

"Look who is talking! Didn't I advise you to stay away from Bob for the time being?"

"That would have meant staying away from you."

Powell hadn't considered the possibility Hayley had returned to work because of his presence. He thought she was a workaholic who couldn't stay away from Bob.

"Would you like to come back to my place after dinner?" Powell asked.

"I like the idea but we need to be up early tomorrow."

"That's easy. I just won't let you go to sleep."

CHAPTER TWENTY

David Jennings became instantly alert. He was sure he had heard the sound of someone walking around downstairs. He probably wouldn't have heard anything if he'd been allowed to carpet the house but his wife was adamant the original floorboards were far too attractive a feature to be hidden away under cheap carpets.

The house was two hundred years old and though the floorboards were probably not original, they were old enough to have recognisable creaks in certain locations. He had heard the familiar sound of the loose floorboard at the bottom of the stairs, creaking under the weight of someone's foot.

There was silence and after a minute, David thought he must have been dreaming. He pulled the quilt tighter around his body. It was dark outside and he didn't like having his sleep disturbed. He needed to be up at six and on the train to London by seven.

The sudden, nervous, adrenaline rush he had felt as a result of suspecting there was an intruder in his house kept him awake. The second time he heard the footsteps on the stairs, he realised he not only had an intruder but he was slowly coming upstairs. At least, David assumed it was a man. Women didn't invade your house in the middle of the night.

David knew he wasn't a brave man. In his thirty three years of life, he'd never been in a fight. He might say he was born to be a lover not a fighter but that had never really been fully put to the test as he'd only ever loved one woman. He had met Liz at university and married young. It was a shock when they discovered they couldn't have children but their love had been a stronger bond than the need for children and they were soon to celebrate their tenth wedding anniversary.

David had eventually told Liz about his experiences as a teenager and the abuse. She had sat and listened and cried. Then she put her arms around him and held him tight. His admission explained many of the problems they had experienced during their married life. It had taken him a long time to open up about his troubled past and having done so he finally felt able to confront those responsible.

David had never thrown a punch in anger and he would go out of his way to avoid confrontation. He was a slim build and lacked any interest in sport. His passion was to write and he hoped one day to generate enough income from his writing to be able to give up the day job as an accountant managing the tax affairs of his clients.

He now understood the saying, frozen with fear, because that was exactly how he felt. His heart was pounding. Perhaps if he pretended to be asleep, the intruder would steal whatever he could find and then leave.

David hadn't heard any further signs of the man's progress up the stairs. He was pleased Liz was spending the weekend with a friend in Nottingham. She was safe but he also missed her strength. She would have already bounded out of bed and confronted the intruder. But she was a kickboxer and he was an accountant.

The fear had obviously paralysed his brain. He should be calling the police not pretending to be asleep. He reached a hand from under his duvet and took his phone from the bedside table. He dialled the number for the emergency services and his call was quickly answered by a female voice, who asked which service he wanted. He quietly asked for the police but before he could say any more, two men rushed into the bedroom brandishing guns.

One of the men held his finger against his lips indicating David should remain quiet while pointing his gun directly at David. The other man moved around the other side of the bed. David slept with his curtains open and the man closed them but not before David identified both men were dressed in black.

David's throat was so dry, he couldn't have called out if he wanted. He had no intention of doing anything to provoke these men. At least they hadn't already shot him, which was a good sign.

Within seconds of entering the bedroom, the first man had pushed the muzzle of his weapon against the side of David's head and covered his mouth with a large hand wearing a leather glove. David found the strong smell of leather disgusting but he didn't struggle.

The second man grabbed the wrist of David's left hand, which had been holding his phone and prised the phone free. He listened for a second before speaking. "Sorry to have bothered you. I thought I had an intruder but it turns out my wife came home a day early. Thanks for your help."

David listened to the man as he reconfirmed everything was okay. How did he manage to remain so calm. This obviously wasn't the first time he'd broken into someone's home. Who were these men?

The intruder finally disconnected the call and turned to the other man. "We'd better hurry. Just in case."

CHAPTER TWENTY ONE

Hayley was in the kitchen and Bob in his study, where he seemed to spend most of his time. Powell was alone in the lounge reading a political biography, which he was finding extremely boring. It had been recommended by Bob as an excellent read but it was proving to be the reading equivalent of watching paint dry. He had a coffee by his side and the evening news was on television in the background.

Powell was considering asking Hayley to sneak upstairs for some excitement before bedtime. He couldn't spend the night with her as he had done forty eight hours earlier. That wouldn't be appropriate in Bob's house but most nights Bob would work until after eleven in his study. Just the thought of disappearing upstairs for a quickie was turning him on. It made him feel a bit like a naughty schoolboy and frankly it was a very exciting idea, made more enticing by the memories of their recent night together, where they had spent little time actually sleeping.

Powell's attention was caught by the local news reporting the death of a man in Brighton. If it had been someone from another city, he wouldn't even have looked up from his book. The man had died of a suspected drug overdose, a sadly all too common occurrence. His body had been found by his wife, who had been staying with friends.

It was the photo of the man, which triggered Powell's memory. He was sure it was the same man he had seen leaving Jack Street's house in the mini. Powell listened more attentively but there was no further information about the circumstances of his death. The news item didn't merit anything except the briefest mention.

Powell wasn't a great believer in coincidences. What was he doing at Jack Street's house? It was possible he worked for Jack but if that was the case, he would have expected the news to mention the fact he was linked to someone so famous and newsworthy.

Jack had been a visitor to Bob's house just two nights ago. Powell was getting uncomfortable vibes about the relationship between Bob and Jack Street. Jack's sexuality was often the subject of the gossip columns. Neither he or Bob had ever been married. Powell had to admit he hadn't any solid reason for his concerns but something didn't seem right.

Powell realised his sighting of the man leaving Jack Street's house amounted to important information, which was pertinent to the inevitable police investigation. The only problem was that neither Jack or Bob might appreciate him interfering. He doubted that the police officers in the following car had seen anything of the man driving the mini as he left the house. Only Powell had a clear view of his face before he sped away.

Powell himself had a bit of a chequered history with the police but he knew he didn't really have a choice. Jack Street needed to explain why the dead man had been at his home. Powell decided he wouldn't let Bob or Hayley know of his intentions until after he had spoken to the police. He didn't want an argument or have to justify his actions. He had two officers sitting outside the house so there was no better time than the present.

When Powell returned to the house, he informed Bob and Hayley about the man he had seen leaving Jack Street's home, who was subsequently found dead. Bob had questioned whether Powell was simply mistaken and Powell conceded it was a possibility but in any event he had informed the police.

Bob hadn't been pleased by the revelation and became quite hostile to Powell but Hayley had chimed in that Powell had done the right thing. Powell was learning that Hayley judged everything by its impact on Bob. The man's death had no fallout for Bob so she didn't have an issue with what Powell had done. He wondered what her reaction would have been if Powell had caused a problem for Bob. It would test their relationship.

Powell understood why Bob was upset but his relationship with

Jack Street was curious. Their age differences meant they hadn't gone to school together but they obviously had a very close bond. Powell wondered how they ever became friends. He would ask Hayley when he could get her on her own.

CHAPTER TWENTY TWO

Powell was happy to have an excuse to leave the house even if it was only to pick up the Chinese takeaway. Unfortunately they didn't deliver but Bob swore it was some of the freshest and best Chinese food he had ever eaten. Hayley endorsed Bob's view and provided thirty pounds in cash as Bob explained the takeaway didn't accept cards. Powell was deeply suspicious of places that didn't accept cards. If they were any good why wouldn't they accept cards? At least he wasn't getting the meal from the nearby Chinese, which looked decidedly uninviting from the outside.

Powell was beginning to question whether he was any longer providing any value as a bodyguard. He was thinking it was about time to recommend to Bob that he hire himself someone new if he still felt the need for additional protection. After dinner, he would bring up the subject of leaving. He could make an excuse about being needed back at the bar.

Powell was bored spending long hours at Bob's house and Bob had become less friendly. He was polite but Powell was aware there had been a slight shift in their relationship. Bob obviously didn't appreciate Powell talking to the police about seeing the man leaving Jack's house. Even the occasional suggestive touch from Hayley as she walked past, wasn't sufficient excitement to stop the time from dragging.

Powell drove down the end of Bob's road feeling a sense of having escaped prison. The feeling was quite intoxicating but would be short lived. It was only a ten minute drive to the Chinese. He turned a sharp bend in the road and checked his rear view mirror. A large black vehicle was speeding up fast behind but he wasn't unduly bothered. He wasn't in any hurry and didn't want a race. There were no other cars on the road and there was plenty of room to overtake.

The severe jolt from the vehicle ramming him from behind was both unexpected and painful. He knew instinctively he had to react fast as to not do so could be terminal. It had been no accidental collision.

He gripped the steering wheel tightly as he didn't want to be pushed off the road. The van had dropped a few yards behind after the first impact but was accelerating again. Powell regretted he was driving Bob's Volvo instead of his own BMW, which would soon leave the van trailing in its wake.

He was ready for the second jolt as his car lurched forward but stayed on the road. At least the Volvo was solidly built. He put his foot to the floor on the accelerator and gained a few yards advantage but it was a short-lived respite. The black van was surprisingly fast for such a large vehicle and within seconds was back on his tail.

Powell was rapidly gaining on a slow moving saloon up ahead. He was about to become the meat in a sandwich if he didn't do something. He needed to ensure whoever was in the car ahead didn't get involved in what was unfurling.

Powell looked through his wing mirror and could see the black van seemed to have changed tactic and instead of ramming was now trying to overtake. The van was alongside the rear of his car and gradually winning the speed battle. It seemed his Volvo was no match for the van in a straight line.

Powell would very shortly be trapped between the car ahead and the van on his side. There was no chance to turn off the road, which was lined with hedges and trees. The road was dry and he knew instinctively what to do. He slammed his foot on the brake and was grateful for modern cars and ABS brakes, which stopped the wheels from locking. He had both hands firmly on the steering wheel as the back end started to slide. He quickly released the brake to avoid skidding and regained control. The van had shot past not expecting his action.

Powell jumped out of the car and ran for a gap in the trees. The van was still coming to a stop about a hundred metres up the road. He had a good head start and fancied his chances more on foot. The occupants of the van were probably armed but Powell wasn't hanging around to find out.

He ran deep into the trees before stopping for a second. He was breathing heavily. He took in oxygen through large breaths and listened for the sounds of pursuit but could hear nothing. Perhaps they had decided not to follow. He took his phone from his pocket and called the cavalry.

The police were quickly at the scene. Powell slowly retraced his steps through the small wood and found three police cars parked near his deserted car. There was no sign of the van.

Powell called Hayley to explain there would be a considerable delay in the delivery of the Chinese as he was being questioned at length by the police. He assured her he was safe and well and would explain the details when he returned.

An hour later, Powell returned to the house to be met by a barrage of questions. He refused to answer any until they had reheated the Chinese in the microwave as he was starving hungry.

Powell recounted events in a straightforward manner without embellishment.

When he finished, Hayley spoke first. "You talk about it like it's an everyday occurrence. Someone tried to kill you."

"Powell is a bodyguard," Bob replied. "It goes with the job."

Hayley shot Bob a disapproving look. "I don't think this was part of the job description."

"They must have thought I was in the car," Bob continued. "Sounds like you had a narrow escape."

"I was lucky this time," Powell agreed. "But we can't be sure it was you they were after. There are people in my past who would throw a party at my demise."

"What did the police say?" Hayley asked.

"Not much," Powell responded. "I was able to give them some of the number plate of the van so hopefully they will be able to trace it but I wouldn't be certain. The police will probably just find the burnt out shell of a van."

"What do we do now?" Hayley quizzed. "I'm scared."

"Actually, I think it's best Bob finds a new bodyguard. Just in case this attack was aimed solely at me. I don't want to add further to Bob's troubles."

Powell had made the decision to leave on the drive back to the house. As Bob's bodyguard, he had to spend every minute at the house. He needed the freedom to discover who was behind the attack with the van.

"You can't leave," Bob stressed. "I need to increase security if anything not have you leave."

"I can recommend a very good alternative. It's someone I know well and he is available immediately. His name is Jenkins and he used to be a paratrooper. We've worked together a few times and I can vouch for him. I'll stay around for a couple more days to effect a handover."

"I'm not happy," Bob replied.

"I'm sorry but I honestly think it's for the best."

"It sounds to me like you're deserting the sinking ship," Bob retorted angrily.

"Bob! That isn't fair," Hayley exclaimed. "Powell's already saved your life at least once."

"I'm sorry," Bob apologised. "These attacks have me right out of my comfort zone. I shouldn't have said that."

"I understand," Powell sympathised. "You don't ever get used to people trying to kill you."

CHAPTER TWENTY THREE

It had been a couple of days since Powell left his job as Bob's bodyguard, having handed over to Jenkins, who was happy with the role and liked the idea of being back in Brighton. Powell was pleased to be able to offer his old friend some well-paid work and to have the opportunity for a few beers together, although they would have to be put on hold until Bob's safety could be guaranteed.

Powell followed the news about Jack Street with interest. A couple of new claims had been made about him being a sexual predator. In a climate where it seemed revelations were being made daily about older celebrities, it did appear to Powell there couldn't be so much smoke without some fire.

He immediately realised that was an unfair thought. The crimes were so abhorrent and the damage to a celebrity's name so damaging, they deserved to be given the benefit of the doubt until something was actually proven. The lurid headlines were the work of newspaper owners desperate to sell newspapers not independent minds concerned with seeking out the truth.

Jack Street was an easy target for anyone who wanted their own fifteen minutes of fame. The police had to investigate any claim of abuse but they would be extra thorough with celebrities, to ensure there was no suspicion they were getting any special treatment. There could be no hint of a cover up where such serious allegations were concerned.

Powell had arranged to meet his friend Brian for dinner. The man who had initially put Powell in contact with Bob. It had been a couple of months since they last met. Brian enjoyed his trips to Powell's bar, which usually involved too much drinking and discussions about how to put the world to right.

Brian worked for the Security Services and had been a source of great help to Powell on several occasions over the last couple of years.

"I'll have a large Scotch," Brian replied when the barman asked what he wanted to drink.

"I'll have the same," Powell said. Then turned back to Brian and asked, "Tough day?"

"Days plural. Every day is the same. We're fighting a losing battle. Too many terrorist threats and eventually we know one of them will succeed."

The barman put the two drinks on the bar. Brian picked up his whisky and immediately took a large drink.

"I better take the bottle," Powell said and the barman handed across the three quarter full bottle of malt whisky. "Let's sit down," Powell suggested and led the way to a table in a discrete corner of the bar.

"It's not like in your day," Brian bemoaned once seated. "The Irish were a piece of cake compared with today's terrorists."

Powell took a large drink of his whisky and for a second remembered the past. The Irish terrorists may not compare but they had still murdered his wife twenty years earlier.

"You should think about retiring," Powell suggested. "I'd say buy a bar but it might not be the best advice. You might drink the profits dry."

"I only drink too much when I meet you," Brian retorted and downed the remainder of his drink. "It's one of the few times I get to let off steam. Other friends don't understand what I do for a living and I have to be guarded in what I say."

"I was only joking, Brian. I wasn't implying you're an alcoholic." Powell refilled both glasses. "Not yet at least."

"What would I do if I retired? I'm not quite fifty. I'm not qualified for much else and if I spent too much time at home, I'd soon have a divorce on my hands."

"You really are in a bad way."

"Speak for yourself. At least I haven't been shot or had anyone try to kill me recently."

"True."

"Speaking of which, I checked out the police reports as you asked and they've made no progress with tracking the van."

"I gave them the first three letters of the number plate. How difficult can it be for them to trace?"

"They seem to have tried a great many combinations of the letters but came up blank. The report says you must have mistaken the letters due to the stress you were under."

"I guess it could have been a completely false number plate. They were definitely professional."

"The police think the attackers mistakenly believed Bob Hale was in your car. After all, you were his bodyguard so you went everywhere together."

"I'm not convinced. They would have to be blind not to realise I was alone in the car."

"Bob could have been hiding out of view. It's what you would have told him to do if he was in the car."

"There were at least two men in the van. The previous attacks on Bob were the work of a lone individual. And I'm sure they knew I was by myself in the car. What did they hope to achieve? If they killed me, Bob would simply recruit more bodyguards. It's not as if I'm irreplaceable."

"Okay so perhaps it isn't linked to Bob Hale," Brian agreed. "You've upset plenty enough other people over the years."

"Top of that list would be certain elements within the CIA," Powell admitted. Eighteen months earlier, Powell had disrupted a covert operation by a rogue element within the CIA.

"It's a possibility," Brian agreed. "Although they normally act out of self-interest not petty revenge. I can't see how you are any threat to them or how they have anything to gain from your death."

"Can you ask around? See what you can find out."

"I'll put some feelers out. Does that mean dinner's on you?"

"At the speed you're consuming my whisky, I'd be more concerned to ensure I'm picking up your bar bill."

Brian refilled the glasses. "A toast," he said, raising his glass. "To friendship."

"To friendship." Powell touched glasses before taking a drink. "You seem more melancholy than usual."

"We lost a man today. I trained him and sent him out to get blown to pieces. There are just scraps of him left to put in the coffin. He was about to become a father for the first time. Now his wife will be a single parent and the child will never know his father."

Powell knew what that was like. While working for MI5 his wife had been murdered and he'd been left alone to bring up his young daughter. He'd left MI5 and purchased the bar in Brighton. It had been a good life until a couple of years earlier when his daughter had also been killed.

"Perhaps you really do need to think about retiring," Powell said.

"No. I just need another drink," Brian replied, picking up the empty bottle. "Anyway, if I retired who would be around to stop you getting yourself killed."

"Let's order some food," Powell suggested. "Do you want steak or fish?"

"Steak please."

"Red or white wine?"

"Red."

"Coming right up," Powell said, rising from his chair. "When I come back I want your opinion on Jack Street."

"Street? You mean the singer?"

"Yes. I think we can add him to the list of people I've pissed off."

CHAPTER TWENTY FOUR

Ed Manners organised the meeting for a private dining club in Mayfair. Crawford was already sat at the table when Ed arrived. A waiter poured them some water and left them with the menus.

"It's a long time since I was last here," Crawford said.

"Well you have been rather persona non grata over here for the last year. Instigating acts of terrorism on our shores doesn't really make you a welcome guest."

"I hope you haven't summoned me here just to receive a lecture," Crawford said in an American accent, which clearly labelled him as someone from New York. "It achieved most of the desired effect. Your parliament has passed laws you couldn't get through before the bombings."

"I don't deny that but didn't bring you here to debate the merits of your previous actions. You're lucky we allowed you back in the country."

"I'm only here for two weeks for the conference."

"The Director General wasn't happy the CIA decided to send you."

"He'll get over it. Tell me, why did you ask me to get rid of Powell. Obviously, I have plenty of reasons to want him dead but why do you want him killed?"

"That's not important."

"I only ask because twelve months ago I was told in no uncertain times by your boss and mine that he and his friends were untouchable."

"This is a matter between you and I. Our bosses don't need to be involved."

"So this is unsanctioned as I suspected?"

"It's become a little irrelevant as your men fucked up."

"We didn't have a great deal of time to plan anything. When you called with the tip he would be leaving the house, we reacted as best as we could in the circumstances. Do you want me to try again?"

"Yes. This time make no mistakes but try to make it look like an accident. I don't want to attract undue attention to his passing."

"And in return?" Crawford asked.

"I didn't think you would need any inducement to want to kill Powell. Not after the trouble he caused you."

"I want Powell dead but other than some personal satisfaction, I don't actually gain anything by his death, whereas I assume you do. There is something I would like in exchange if you want me to finish the job?"

"What?"

"I want you to help me locate George Broderick."

"Who the hell is he?"

"He's been hacking into our computers and needs to be stopped urgently. We don't want another long drawn out extradition problem so we would like some help shortcutting the process."

"What do you mean?"

"We want him picked up and put on a plane to the States."

"What has he discovered?"

"We doubt he even knows what he's stumbled across but we need to ensure it goes no further."

"Why don't you just silence him permanently?"

"We would like to interrogate him to be sure he's working alone. We might even like to put his skills to use working for us."

"Okay, I can help with your problem if you are willing to deal with Powell."

"How urgent is Powell?" Crawford asked.

"Not desperately urgent. It's more important to get it right this time."

"Then we have a deal," Crawford agreed.

CHAPTER TWENTY FIVE

Powell had told Afina to take the night off and join him, Jenkins and Mara for a night out. The bar could survive a night without its manager as the assistant manager was very capable, having been well trained by Afina. Powell wanted to let his hair down with his best friends.

No longer working for Bob already had its advantages. He stayed in bed later than usual, went to the gym for a serious workout and then caught up with paying bills. None of which would have been possible if still in Bob's employ. Most importantly, he could decide to go out for the evening without first having to check Bob's plans. Life was returning to normal.

Powell chose an Indian in the centre of town, renowned for its quality food. It would be an expensive night but it had been a long time since they had all been out together. They were all coming from different directions and agreed to meet at the restaurant.

Powell took a taxi from home, which dropped him at the end of the road where the restaurant was located, which was pedestrianised. He arrived at the same moment as Mara. They exchanged kisses and went inside to be joined a short time later by Afina and then Jenkins.

Powell ordered a bottle of Prosecco and some Poppadoms while they caught up on each other's news.

"How come you have a night off?" Powell asked Jenkins.

"Bob was going to a party somewhere. I tried to insist I should go with him but he was having none of it. Told me to take the night off so here I am choosing to spend it with my three favourite people in Brighton."

"We're the only people you know in Brighton," Afina replied.

"Which is why you are my favourite people," Jenkins answered and everyone laughed.

"Bob is always attending private parties. It wasn't at Jack Street's by any chance?" Powell asked.

"Does he know Jack Street?" Jenkins asked, surprised.

"They are close friends," Powell confirmed.

"Who is Jack Street?" Afina asked.

"He's a singer," Jenkins explained. "Crap but very famous and old enough to be Powell's father."

"No one's that old," Afina joked."

"Thanks," Powell replied. "Age is just a number."

"That is so true, "Mara agreed. "I had a client in his seventies last week. He was a bit like you, Powell."

"I'm nowhere near my bloody seventies," Powell retorted.

"I didn't mean similar in age."

"Was he a kickboxer?"

"No but he was in great shape and he was very polite. He spoke proper English just like you and he was also very religious like you."

"I'm not religious."

"Really, I always thought you were. I remember you kept saying, God that feels good. Oh God don't stop."

Jenkins and Afina burst into a fit of laughter.

"Very funny," Powell said, helping himself to a drink of wine. "With friends like you lot who needs enemies."

"Well you've more than your share of them," Jenkins said. "Any more idea who was in the van?"

"What van?" Afina quickly asked.

Jenkins gave Powell a look of apology, realising he'd said the wrong thing.

"It was nothing much," Powell explained. "A van banged into my rear while I was driving Bob's car. I stopped but he drove off."

"So it was just a traffic accident?" Afina asked.

Powell didn't believe in lying to Afina. "I think the van was trying to push me off the road but didn't make a very good job of it."

"You mean someone was trying to kill you?" Afina asked, not

sounding entirely surprised.

"It looks that way," Powell replied.

"Why?"

"That's the million dollar question. I'm honestly not sure."

Powell was pleased the waiter chose that moment to ask for their orders. Neither Afina or Mara had much experience of eating Indian food so both asked Powell to order for them.

Much of the conversation over dinner centred around how they all met and their adventures. After two hours they were ready to find a bar to continue the evening.

Mara suggested a place, which was less than five minutes distance. It included a dance floor, which everyone except Powell thought was a good idea. There were no tables free so they stood at the bar and ordered a variety of drinks. Jenkins and Powell had a beer while the girls ordered another bottle of Prosecco.

After a short while the girls encouraged Powell and Jenkins to join them on the dance floor, which was heaving with bodies. Powell did his less than impressive dancing on the spot routine, while the others rather more enthusiastically moved around to the music.

They had been dancing for about five minutes when Powell realised that Mara was dancing with Jenkins and Afina had been joined by a young man, leaving him on his own. He felt a little self-conscious as he was both by himself and twice as old as most of the other dancers. He didn't want to be mistaken for a sad old git and was about to call it a day, when an attractive woman in a bright red dress came to his aid.

She had been on the periphery of his vision, seemingly dancing with no one in particular. She was probably in her early thirties, with long, blonde hair and the short dress revealed long, toned legs. All in all, it was a very sexy package and when she smiled at him there was no way he was going to leave the dance floor.

He smiled and said simply, "I'm Powell."

He couldn't hear her reply, the music was so loud it was impossible to hear anything anyone said. He danced a little, making an effort not to do his usual impersonation of a statue. The pretty blonde was a good dancer and had a feline grace as she moved in time to the music.

When the song finished, he indicated the bar and the need for a drink. He was pleased she decided to join him.

"What would you like?" Powell asked.

"Vodka and red bull, please."

He ordered her drink and another beer for himself. He paid for the drinks and handed over her glass.

"Thanks, Powell. Do you come here often?"

His mind was dulled with an evening of alcohol but he wasn't drunk. He became alert and glanced around to locate the others. They seemed happily dancing so he turned back to the blonde.

"I didn't get your name."

"Sam. Short for Samantha if you prefer."

This time Powell clearly heard the response and detected the American accent.

"Sam sounds good to me. And I come here very rarely. What about you?"

"My first time."

"Are you here by yourself?"

"I came with my boyfriend but he wanted to leave and I didn't. I don't suppose you fancy going on somewhere else? Just in case he decides to come back." She smiled a smile that nine times out of ten would get her own way.

"I'm here with friends," Powell replied.

"Can't I tempt you?" Sam asked. "I think we could have a load of fun tonight."

"Maybe later."

The others finished dancing and joined them at the bar. They ordered more of the same drinks plus Jager shots for everyone. Powell made the introductions to Sam.

"I need the bathroom," Powell said to Sam. He turned to Jenkins and said, "This heat is a bitch. I need a piss."

Jenkins took a second to register what he had heard. Powell wasn't surprised as it had been getting on for two years since they worked in Saudi Arabia and established the coded phrase as a way of letting the other know, they urgently needed to say something in private.

"I could do with a pee," Jenkins said. "I'll come with you."

"Look after Sam," Powell said to Mara and Afina as he walked away, closely followed by Jenkins.

"What the hell is wrong?" Jenkins asked, once they were inside the toilets and after Powell checked the cubicles were empty.

"I think Sam is trying to pick me up."

"Lucky you," Jenkins replied, smiling. "She's a stunner."

"I'm not sure her motives are entirely romantic."

"So just give her a shag and enjoy yourself."

"That's not what I meant. She knew my name."

"You didn't tell her?"

"I did but it was virtually impossible to hear me. I'm sure she already knew it."

"She has an American accent," Jenkins stated.

"She does indeed. I may be wrong but I suspect she has an ulterior motive for suggesting we go somewhere else."

"What should we do?"

"Nothing. I'm not going anywhere with her but we need to be alert when we leave, just in case there is a nasty surprise waiting for us outside."

They rejoined the others and after a few minutes, Mara and Afina were trying to drag Jenkins back on the dance floor, despite his protestations he was tired.

"Go dance," Powell encouraged. "It's not every day you get asked by two beautiful women." Powell reasoned Jenkins had been unwilling to leave him alone but he felt quite safe with Sam. He was pretty certain if there was to be a problem, it would be when they left the bar.

"I like your friends," Sam said. "They are an interesting mix."

"They certainly are. Do you want another drink?"

"I'm fine thanks. Actually, I need to visit the bathroom."

Powell wondered if Sam had left to report her failure to get him to leave with her and come up with a new plan. Or was he just being paranoid? After a minute, he decided to follow her to the toilet. If he saw her on the phone his suspicions would be confirmed.

There were too many women going in and out of the toilets for him to contemplate sneaking a look inside. In fact, he received a couple of strange looks from girls who passed because he was the only man loitering in an otherwise all-female area. Feeling conspicuous and having achieved nothing, he was about to walk away when Sam emerged from the toilet.

"You're in the wrong place," she said. The surprise on her face quickly turned to a smile.

"I thought I might grab a kiss or something while my friends weren't looking."

"It's probably a bit busy here for the something but a kiss is a good idea." Sam stepped close and pulling him near arched her neck. He accepted the invitation and kissed her gently on the lips.

Despite the presence of girls pushing past on either side, she kissed him back passionately. Powell enjoyed the sensation but was imagining it was Hayley he was kissing.

"Get a room," one stranger suggested, good naturedly.

Sam broke the clinch and smiled. "Would you like perhaps to reconsider going somewhere else with me?"

"I'm sorry but I can't leave my friends. That wouldn't be right. We haven't been out together for ages."

"In that case I'll have that drink you offered."

CHAPTER TWENTY SIX

As the evening wore on, Powell wasn't one hundred per cent sure there was anything sinister about Sam. She was good company and had a credible back story, which could be real but equally if she was working undercover, he would expect her to have nothing less.

When it came time to leave, Powell was in two minds about how to proceed. He had spent some time considering the options and decided the most important factor was to ensure the safety of Afina and Mara. He didn't know what lay in wait outside but wanted to confront it alone.

"Would you like to come back to my place?" Powell asked Sam.

She smiled broadly, obviously surprised by the suggestion. "That would be the perfect end to a fun evening."

Powell noticed Jenkins giving him a quizzical look. "See the girls get home safely, Jenkins. I'm going to take Sam back to my place."

"Lucky you," Mara said, looking Sam up and down appreciatively. "I don't suppose you want any extra company?" Then she laughed and added, "Only kidding."

"No you're not," Afina laughed, slapping Mara on the back. "But I think you're out of luck tonight."

"I need to pay a visit to the bathroom before I leave," Sam announced.

Powell wasn't surprised. He had expected his invitation would cause Sam to want to make contact with someone outside the bar and provide an update. The sudden need to visit the bathroom could be innocent but he wouldn't put much money on the fact.

Once Sam had left, Powell pulled Jenkins aside and quickly explained his plan.

Jenkins nodded his agreement. "I'll put the girls in a taxi and then take one back to your place," he said as they rejoined the others.

"I thought you were taking Sam home?" Afina asked.

"Sam may not be all she appears," Powell replied with a serious expression.

"But…"

"I don't have time to explain," Powell interrupted. "I want you to spend the night at Mara's. Please just do as I ask and leave now."

"Let's go," Mara encouraged, pulling on Afina's sleeve. "Powell knows what he is doing."

"Call me first thing in the morning," Afina demanded. Then she turned and headed for the exit with the others quickly following behind.

Sam returned after a couple of minutes. "Where did everyone go?"

"They all went back to Mara's."

"So we are finally on our own?"

"Unless your boyfriend is waiting outside for you."

"He won't be."

"I hope you're right."

"He's just someone I met online. He's not really my boyfriend. It was just our second and last date."

"Shall we get going then?"

"Lead the way."

Powell glanced around as they left the bar, trying not to look as if he suspected imminent trouble. With many others spilling out on to the pavement at the same time, he didn't really expect trouble in front of so many potential witnesses but he was going to take nothing for granted.

He saw nothing to cause concern as they walked the short distance to the taxi rank. There was a small queue but no sign of Jenkins and the girls. There were plenty of taxis despite it being after two in the morning and within a few minutes they were at the front of the queue. Powell opened the rear door for Sam to get in and then told the driver where to go through his half open window, before joining Sam in the back of the taxi. Sam sat close and leaned her head on his shoulder. The journey took only ten minutes.

"We're here," he announced as the taxi slowed to a halt.

Sam looked out of the window with a slightly quizzical expression. "This is where you live?"

"Not exactly. It's the bar I own. I have an apartment upstairs."

"But I was so looking forward to seeing where you live."

Powell thought Sam seemed flustered. He paid the driver and stepped out of the taxi.

"Are you coming?" he asked as Sam hesitated.

She climbed out of the taxi and stood on the pavement taking in her surroundings as the taxi drove off. "Where are we exactly?"

"Hove." Powell opened the bar, turned off the alarm and led the way inside. "What do you think?"

"Well I guess you're never short of a drink."

"Speaking of which, why don't I open a bottle of champagne."

"Champagne's good for me."

Powell took a bottle of quality champagne from the cold box behind the bar and picked up two glasses.

"Let's go upstairs," he suggested.

He led the way to what was in fact Afina's living room.

"Take a seat," he said, indicating the sofa. He stayed standing as he placed the glasses on the coffee table in front of the sofa and started opening the champagne bottle.

"Can I use your bathroom?" Sam asked. "I need to make room for the champagne."

"It's the door at the other end of the hallway."

"Thanks."

Powell was pretty certain she would shortly be on the phone again but didn't bother following.

When she returned he had poured the champagne and offered Sam a glass.

"This wasn't how I expected my evening to end," Powell smiled.

"Me neither," Sam agreed. "But the evening isn't finished yet."

Powell touched glasses, "To new friends."

"To new friends," Sam repeated and tasted her champagne. "That's very nice."

"It's vintage. A bit like me."

Powell's phone rang and he took it from his trouser pocket. "It's Jenkins," he announced before pressing the phone to his ear. "Hi. Everything all right?"

"There's a black van parked up at the end of your road. I think it's safe to assume they were the welcoming committee."

"I thought you lot were going straight to bed?" Powell replied, mindful Sam was listening.

"Hang on, the van's on the move. Did Sam have a chance to make a call yet?"

"Yes. Sam is here with me."

"I'll get there as soon as I can."

"Thanks. I suggest you all get to bed or you are going to have very sore heads in the morning."

"Take care. They are almost certain to be armed."

"I always take precautions." Powell looked at Sam with raised eyebrows. "Don't call again, I'll be busy." He ended the call. "Sorry about that. They are all drunk and checking up on us."

"How do you all come to be friends?" Sam asked.

"Afina and Jenkins have worked for me and Mara is Afina's best friend."

"They sure know how to have a good time. Speaking of which, I've seen the lounge and the bathroom. Are you going to show me the bedroom?"

"It's the door next to the bathroom. I need to go make sure everything is locked up properly. You go ahead and make yourself comfortable. I'll be with you in one minute."

CHAPTER TWENTY SEVEN

Powell headed downstairs as Sam entered the bedroom. He had wanted to come back to the bar for a number of reasons, not least because he kept a gun downstairs in his office. He collected the weapon and checked his CCTV, which showed no activity outside the bar.

He didn't expect Sam's friends to come charging straight into the bar. They would almost certainly take their time and wait until Sam had done her job, which was presumably to shag him senseless so he was asleep when they arrived. She was probably on the phone to them right now finalising details.

Powell unlocked the rear entrance to the bar and returned upstairs to the bedroom. He opened the door and for a second forgot all thoughts of the woman on the bed being complicit in trying to end his life. Sam was sprawled out on the bed wearing matching black underwear and looked as seductive an image as he'd ever experienced.

"I hope you like what you see," Sam smiled.

Powell stood transfixed at the end of the bed wondering if it was too mad a notion to have sex with Sam, while he still had the opportunity. She would be good. He had no doubt on that score.

A little reluctantly, he forced himself to focus on the reality of his situation. He took his gun from behind his back, where it had been tucked into his trouser belt.

Sam took a second to register the presence of the weapon and then she smiled. "Please don't hurt me, Sir. I'll do anything you want," she pleaded in an over acting tone of voice.

"I'm sure you would until your friends arrive."

"What friends?"

"You could at least pretend to be a little scared," Powell said.

"Why? That isn't a real gun. Is it?"

"It's more real than you are."

"What do you need a gun for? I'm lying on your bed in my underwear. You got lucky tonight. Or do you want to role play a rape scenario? That could be fun."

"You're quite an actress."

There was a small knock on the door and Jenkins entered.

"This could be fun," Sam said. "You should have said if you wanted to get kinky."

Jenkins was staring appreciatively at Sam's body.

"Anyone see you?" Powell asked, prodding his arm to get his attention.

"No. They must be out front somewhere. I came through the back."

"Where's your phone?" Powell demanded of Sam.

She ignored his question. "This is getting beyond a joke. I think I'm going to leave." She started to move to the edge of the bed.

"You are going nowhere," Powell insisted and aimed his gun in line with Sam's knee.

"You aren't going to shoot me," Sam said.

"That's a very big assumption to make in your situation."

"I don't think you are the type to kill a woman."

Powell stared hard at Sam. "Who said anything about killing you? I'm just going to cripple your knee. Now, behave yourself or you will be spending even more time than usual on your back. "

Sam hesitated, pulled her knees up close and wrapped her arms around her legs. "What now?"

"Your phone, please."

"It's in my bag."

Powell could see the bag on the floor beside the bed. "Move across to the other side of the bed," he instructed.

Sam shuffled across the bed. Then Jenkins moved forward and warily picked up her bag from the floor. He soon found the phone and passed it to Powell.

"Password?" Powell asked.

Sam stared straight ahead, ignoring the question.

"It's only going to confirm what I already know," Powell continued. "You don't get paid to be a hero. Give me the password or suffer the consequences." Powell picked up a pillow from the bed and held it in front of the gun so it would muffle the sound of the shot. "You will tell me after I shoot you in one knee and threaten to do the same to the other knee. Save yourself a load of pain."

Sam seemed persuaded he was serious. "060882," she finally answered.

"Your birthday?" Powell asked. "Didn't you learn anything during training? CIA standards are definitely slipping."

"It was a long time ago," Sam answered, not bothering to deny she was CIA trained.

Powell quickly checked for messages and found final proof he hadn't been mistaken. "Sam, I'm disappointed in you. We've only just met but you seem to be already carrying on with someone else." There were several messages sent throughout the evening with updates of her situation.

"Fuck you," Sam swore.

"That's not very ladylike," Powell replied. "Jenkins, I think we need to secure Samantha."

CHAPTER TWENTY EIGHT

Powell called Brian and woke him up from his sleep to ask for help. Powell wanted him to speak to the police as it would carry more weight and get a faster response. A short time later Powell received a call from a senior police officer and explained his plan. The officer had no objections. Brian had obviously given him a five star reference.

Jenkins had tied Sam's hands behind her back and it was time to ask some questions.

"How many men can we expect?" Powell asked.

Sam showed no inclination to answer.

"I have to warn you I am fast losing my patience. I am getting very fed up with Americans trying to kill me. I reckon we have an hour with you, Sam. That would be the minimum time your friends would expect us to spend fucking. You can pass that time pleasantly by answering my questions or you can choose to spend the time in agony. The choice is yours but either way you will answer my questions."

Sam remained quiet but her eyes revealed her nervousness.

"I believe Americans are very fond of Waterboarding," Jenkins said.

"That's a good idea," Powell agreed. "I believe Sam works for the CIA so I'm sure she will be familiar with the technique. She may even have been subjected to it during her training. I believe the average CIA agent lasted ten seconds before they were screaming like babies." Powell allowed his words to sink in before asking again, "How many men are there outside?"

Sam turned her head to the side and said nothing.

"I don't think she's taking us seriously," Jenkins commented.

"Sam, I don't know how much background you were given on me.

I assume you know I used to work for MI5?" From Sam's reaction he guessed she hadn't known. "I'm not the bad guy around here. I pissed off someone senior in your organisation and they are after revenge. This operation of yours is not sanctioned by your Director and the shit is going to hit the fan when this gets out. You will probably be assigned to admin duties in some out of the way arsehole of a place you will hate. That's if you aren't fired for incompetence."

"You tell a good story," Sam finally spoke.

"That's better, Sam. You're remembering your training. Engage with the person interrogating you and do nothing antagonistic. Do you know someone called Crawford?" Powell saw the recognition in her eyes. "He is behind your operation. He wants me dead. I pissed him off about a year back. This is personal for him. You didn't sign up to be used by the likes of Crawford for his personal agenda."

"I just follow orders. I leave decision making to others."

"But you seem like a bright girl, Sam. You can make a decision to save yourself a load of pain."

Sam said nothing.

"Jenkins, go get me a thin towel from the bathroom. Then get us a few bottles of water from the bar."

Jenkins left the bedroom.

"We aren't playing around," Powell cautioned. "It's not as if I'm asking you for state secrets. I just want answers to a few simple questions."

Gaining no response, Powell remained silent until Jenkins returned carrying a towel and three large bottles of water.

Powell turned on the television. It had a wide range of channels and he turned to a channel playing music videos. There was nobody living on either side of the bar so he turned up the volume quite loud.

"A bit of music always adds to the occasion, don't you think?" Powell asked. He didn't want her friends outside to hear her screams if she should start calling out for help.

"That's crap," Jenkins said, referring to the song that started playing.

"You hold her down," Powell said. "Position her sideways across the bed so her head is hanging over the end."

Jenkins pulled Sam in to position. Her face was hanging over the edge of the bed. It was important her head was lower than her body so she didn't actually drown. She tried to resist by kicking out but Jenkins sat on her stomach and used his weight to push back on her shoulders and hold her down. With her hands tied behind her back there was little she could do to resist further.

Powell moved to the side of the bed. He took the towel and placed it over her face, covering her mouth and nose. She tried shaking her head from side to side but Powell gripped her hair and held her head in place. He opened the first bottle of water and poured it over Sam's face, making sure it ran into her nose and mouth. She tried to close her mouth but then her nose filled with water and she opened her mouth to breathe. In her position across the bed, the water filled her throat, mouth and sinuses with water, simulating drowning although the lungs were actually free of water.

The reaction from Sam was immediate as she started to panic and gurgle, trying without success to force the water from her head. After a few seconds, Powell stopped pouring the water and lifted Sam's head so she could breath.

"Please don't," Sam begged once she had recovered.

"Correct me if I'm mistaken but didn't you come here to kill me?" Powell said conversationally. "I want answers to my questions."

He started to push her head back down again and tip his bottle of water.

"Okay. Okay. I'll tell you whatever you want to know."

Powell released his grip on her hair and removed the towel.

"You have one chance to get this right," Powell warned. "If for a second I think you aren't being honest, I'll start again and it will be twice as long as last time."

"There are two men outside," she volunteered.

"That's a good start. Do you work for the CIA?"

"Not directly. We are private contractors working on their behalf.

We all used to work for them in the past and went freelance."

"That makes sense. You are in a pile of trouble because the CIA will deny all knowledge of you. You are looking at a long term in jail."

"Maybe."

"Sam, you need to get real. Your friends aren't going to charge in here and rescue you. You are on your own. You need to cooperate with me and the police."

"What do you want to know?"

"I asked you earlier but you didn't answer. Do you know someone called Crawford, who definitely does work for the CIA?"

"He briefed us on the mission."

"You met him?"

"I saw him but it was Shaw, he's outside in the van, who he briefed. He's my boss."

"Where did you meet him?"

"Regents park."

Powell had confirmation Crawford was in London. "Do you have a contact number for Crawford?"

"No. Shaw will have that."

Powell continued to ask questions for a further twenty minutes. He then called Brian and gave him an update. Brian promised to track down Crawford and put an end to the attacks. He would speak with his Director first thing in the morning.

Next, Powell typed out a message on Sam's phone, saying he was asleep and in twenty minutes she would open the front door. The message also directed whoever was at the other end that the bedroom was the door at the top of the stairs on the right, which was in fact the lounge. That was just a precaution in case someone made it up the stairs.

The message also told them to wait a further ten minutes after she opened the front door to give her time to return to the bedroom. As she wasn't going to be meeting them downstairs that was essential.

Powell went downstairs and opened the front door. He was careful to stay behind the blinds so he couldn't be identified from outside. He grabbed a bottle of whisky from the bar on the way back upstairs. In the bedroom he took a large swig from the bottle and then passed it to Jenkins.

At the appointed time, all hell broke loose downstairs. Powell could hear shouting and the crashing of doors. This was quickly followed by the sound of shots being fired. After a minute there was silence.

Powell's phone rang and the police Inspector, who he had spoken to earlier, announced the downstairs was secure and they should come downstairs with their hands in the air. Powell explained they had a prisoner and it was agreed she would descend first, closely followed by Powell.

Everything went smoothly and Sam was taken away by two burly, armed police officers wearing body protection. One of the CIA men from outside had been shot but would live. Powell was advised the bar was a crime scene and he couldn't just go back to bed so they went back to his house. They took a spare bottle of whisky with them and Powell sent Afina a message to say everything was okay. It had been a long night.

CHAPTER TWENTY NINE

Alex was shocked how easy it was to find a solution to a supposedly difficult problem. A phone call to the Beast's office number was more in hope than expectation of achieving anything. Alex wasn't even sure if the call would be answered. However, a very friendly woman answered and Alex explained the need to speak to the MP about the impact of Brexit on a Croatian living in Britain. The woman apologised for the fact there were no constituency surgeries planned for the immediate future and explained it was because of the dreadful attack on the MP. She thought it unlikely there would be a surgery within the next two weeks.

Alex casually asked if the MP was recovering and the woman confirmed he was and would in fact be undertaking his first public appearance the very next day. The MP was going to attend the unveiling of a memorial to people killed in the recent terrorist bombings. The guest of honour was the Prince of Wales and Alex realised the security would be tight but the target would leave his home and be out in the open. It was the best possible opportunity. Alex thanked the woman for her help and wished the MP a speedy recovery.

The location of the memorial was on the seafront, halfway between the pier and hotel, the two places worst hit by the attacks. Alex knew about the attacks. Even in Croatia it had been front page news. Alex had twenty four hours to prepare.

Alex checked out of the London hotel and loaded the bag into the boot of the hire car. The drive to Brighton took almost two and a half hours, which was twice the time the route planner had said it would take. The M25 motorway was like a giant car park and by the time Alex finally reached the edge of Brighton, frustration had reached maximum levels.

Alex decided to park in the station car park, where leaving a car overnight wouldn't attract any attention. As Alex left the station and walked towards town, it was difficult to forget Linda lived very close. Just for a second, Alex was tempted to make a detour but increased speed. Alex needed to focus on the job in hand. Distractions could get you killed.

Alex was a little dismayed upon arriving at the seafront. Police were already in evidence as barriers were being built around where the event was to take place. A sign on the roadside announced the road would be closed for three hours the next morning, while the ceremony took place. With the large number of dignitaries in attendance, they were taking no chances of a further terrorist attack. Although the presence of royalty might increase security, the main focus of concern would surely be the Prince of Wales not a mere MP. At least Alex was hoping that would be the case.

Alex had thought about laying in weight for the Beast somewhere along the route from his house but decided against the idea. The immediate roads around his house afforded no opportunity and Alex couldn't even be sure he wouldn't arrive by train. Given the likely large volume of traffic on the roads, the train would make sense.

Alex couldn't deal with uncertainty. The event itself offered the one definite opportunity for a distance shot, where it was possible to plan with some certainty. The Beast would be out in the open. Alex was confident the Beast wouldn't want to disappoint royalty by not turning up at the last moment. As the local MP, he had to be present whatever the danger.

Alex was still dressed in a smart suit and didn't look anything like the clown or the assailant with the large moustache, who had previously attacked the MP. It was doubtful the police had any idea what Alex truly looked like.

Alex confidently crossed the road and entered the large hotel opposite the memorial site. Alex wasn't entirely surprised to learn the hotel was fully booked. In fact, the man behind the front desk announced there wasn't a room to be had anywhere in town because of the royal visit. Even the very expensive suites were all taken.

Alex visited several other suitable hotels on the off chance someone had cancelled at the last minute but without success. Alex wasn't surprised. Life was rarely so simple. The hotels would have made a good location for a sniper shot but it was going to be necessary to find an alternative location. Alex surveyed the local buildings from the sea front and one in particular seemed suitable.

CHAPTER THIRTY

Twenty four hours after surviving the CIA attempt on his life, Powell was forced to remember the episode in his life that had caused Crawford to want him dead in the first place. Powell hoped Brian and MI5 would deal with Crawford. He'd been kicked out of the country once before but Sam had admitted to meeting him recently in London. How had he managed to weasel his way back into the country?

Powell wondered how Crawford would react to this latest setback. There was the distinct possibility Crawford might just redouble his efforts. He could call on vast CIA resources. It was imperative MI5 acted quickly. For all Powell knew, there could already be a second team tasked with finishing the job.

Powell wasn't entirely looking forward to the unveiling ceremony. It brought back too many bad memories. Despite his best efforts, Lara and many others had lost their lives. Crawford had been partially responsible for those deaths. When he should have been combatting terrorism, he was actually encouraging it to help justify increased budgets for the CIA.

Now he was again inappropriately using CIA resources to support his own private agenda. Powell knew Crawford wasn't unique. There was something different about those who joined the CIA or its equivalent in other countries. They seemed to think they had a licence to operate outside the law. It made Powell angry that they acted like criminals, justifying their actions as in the national interest.

Powell hadn't been offered any special form of recognition for his part in stopping the terrorism. Lara had rightly received a posthumous medal but his role wasn't publicly acknowledged. To recognise his involvement would be to admit to the part played by rogue sections of the American and British governments. He didn't mind. He didn't want the publicity or medals.

Powell had closed the bar for the morning so anyone who wanted could attend the ceremony or at least watch it on television. He intended to stand with thousands of others in Madeira Drive, watching the giant screen, which was more commonly used to show important sports events. He could have stayed at home and watched on television but then he wouldn't feel part of the event. He felt he was representing Lara by attending. He was pleased her name would permanently feature on the base of the memorial alongside the other victims of the terrorism. Powell would walk past it from time to time and say hello to her memory.

He had a taxi drop him about a mile from the event. It was as near as you could get in a car despite there still being over an hour to the start of the event. The weather was pleasant so the walk was no hardship. He had thought Afina might want to go with him but she had preferred not to be reminded of how close she came to death. Afina had been on the pier with Mara and been forced to jump into the sea to escape a terrorist.

As he came close to the seafront location, Powell found himself surrounded by a large number of other people heading in the same direction. Despite the tragic circumstances being remembered, everyone seemed in good spirits. Whole families seemed to have taken to the streets. It was a demonstration by the people of Brighton that they would not be cowed by the threat of terrorism.

As Powell reached the seafront, the police were guiding them in an orderly queue towards Marina Drive. There was no further space to watch the event close up. Jenkins had offered him the chance to provide extra security to Bob, which would have put him close to the stage but he had declined. If he accepted money to protect Bob, he wouldn't be able to relax and remember events in his own way. After the ceremony, he intended to head straight for a nearby bar and sink a couple of beers. He didn't want to be at the beck and call of Bob.

CHAPTER THIRTY ONE

As there were no hotel rooms available, Alex had spent the night with Linda. She had been busy in the early part of the evening so Alex had arrived at her place at eleven. She was shocked by the change in appearance but approved of the new, smart look. She thought Alex looked every inch the business executive.

Alex had brought a bottle of champagne to share but explained it would be different to the last visit. Alex needed a proper night's sleep. There was a very important business meeting the next day and Alex needed to be sober and out of the house by eight. Linda's only reaction was to comment, in that case, they shouldn't waste time.

The sex had been as good or even better than the previous occasion as they were more relaxed with each other. Linda knew what Alex enjoyed and didn't stint on anything. She kissed passionately and nothing was rushed as she delivered up a mixture of pain and pleasure. Alex was fairly certain she had an orgasm but having recently seen the film 'When Harry met Sally', Alex wouldn't ever again be able to swear with absolute certainty that any woman wasn't acting.

Alex had a shower and bade farewell to Linda at 8.15am. The ceremony was due to take place at 11am. It was probably a good thing Alex didn't expect to return to Brighton any time soon as Linda could become quite addictive. She was an expensive vice compared to cigarettes, especially on a soldier's pay.

Alex walked to the Churchill Square car park, where dressed as a clown it had been necessary to scare the woman half to death while stealing her car. Alex had relocated the hire car from the station after coming up with a new plan. The streets were busy with people going about their business. Alex guessed many people were in town hoping to catch a glimpse of royalty. The weather was perfect for what Alex had in mind. It was a clear, bright morning with little wind.

When Alex reached the car park, it was already full, which was no issue. Alex's car had looked a little lonely the previous evening. Alex took the stairs to the top floor, which looked out towards the seafront. Alex checked for the presence of police on each floor but there was no visible police presence. There would undoubtedly be plenty of security personnel about not wearing uniforms but Alex saw nothing to cause immediate alarm.

Alex didn't immediately approach the car in case anyone was keeping it under observation. It was still in the same place Alex had left it, which was some form of positive. Then again, if the police had become suspicious about the car they probably would leave it in place to try and trap the driver. Alex walked in a large semi-circle around the car and was happy it wasn't receiving any special attention. Then Alex went off to find breakfast, which was more to kill time than out of hunger. The shopping centre wouldn't open until 9am so Alex visited a coffee shop opposite the entrance to the shopping centre.

Sitting at a table in the window, watching the flood of humans walking past, Alex cursed at the realisation of having underestimated the importance of the event. The whole city seemed to be headed towards the seafront, intent on getting a glimpse of a real live Prince. Alex noticed a few more police officers than usual patrolling the streets. Mostly they were being stopped by members of the public and no doubt asked for directions or where to get the best vantage point to see the Prince.

Alex checked his watch, which showed it was time to make a move. If the actual ceremony was due to start at 11am then you could expect the guests to be in place well ahead of time. Alex paid a quick visit to a clothes shop inside the shopping centre and purchased a couple of shirts. Alex was surprised when being told it was necessary to pay for a bag. The British had some strange laws. As Alex took the escalator to the top floor and emerged into the car park, there was nothing to distinguish Alex from any other regular shopper returning from a shopping trip.

Alex glanced around but although there were people going to and from their cars, there seemed to be no cause for alarm. Alex walked to the car, unlocked it and threw the bag on the back seat. Alex moved to the front of the car and peered over the wall in the direction of the sea. There was a clear view of where the event was to take place. A helicopter passed overhead sweeping the area for signs of danger, causing Alex to hurriedly turn away from the wall.

Looking back at the car park, Alex knew it was going to be necessary to act quickly. There wasn't going to be time to leisurely line up the target in the scope before shooting. At any time, the owner of a car parked nearby could return to his car and cause a problem. Alex had no intention of shooting anyone except the target.

Alex went to the boot of the car and removed the telescopic sight from the rifle. Returning to the wall, Alex used the scope to survey the sea front. It was a bit like looking down on an ants nest. The plaque that was to be unveiled was on the promenade facing inwards towards the city. The dignitaries were sat in two rows of chairs facing the sea. Further back, the public were being held behind barriers with a ring of police officers facing the crowd.

Alex could see no sign of the guest of honour but after a minute located the target, sat in the front row. It wasn't going to be an easy shot. There was no cover for taking the shot and the helicopter could return at any time. It would have helped if the target wasn't sitting in front of someone several inches taller. Even so, it was possible to make the shot. The target leaned to each side to speak with the people sitting next to him and each time it afforded a shot at the side of his head.

Alex looked around the car park. Now was as good a time as any. Alex leaned inside the car and pulled the handle to release the bonnet. Walking back to the front of the car, Alex raised the bonnet, which would obscure the view of most people in the car park.

With the bonnet in place, Alex went to the boot of the car and took out the rifle. Alex rested the rifle on the wall and replaced the scope.

It took a few seconds to line up the target.

Alex fired and could see the bullet hit the concrete to the side of the target, throwing up chips of concrete. Alex swore and lined up a second shot. The scope was hopelessly wrong. Alex had aimed six inches to the left of where the bullet hit so this time made an adjustment for the scope.

Through the scope, Alex could see the panic below. Alex squeezed the trigger just as someone sent his target crashing to the ground. The bullet again missed its intended target but hit the trailing leg of the man who had saved the target.

Alex knew there wouldn't be time for a third shot. It was necessary to get away. As Alex slammed the bonnet shut, there was the sound of the helicopter getting nearer. It was heading in Alex's direction so standing in the open holding a rifle wasn't a good idea.

Alex placed the rifle on the ground, hoping it hadn't been seen from the helicopter. Perhaps it would fly past. Alex took a couple of paces toward the driver side door. The helicopter was now directly overhead and any lingering doubts about its purpose were dispelled when a voice boomed out, telling him to get on the ground.

Alex dived behind the wheel of the car and slammed the gears into reverse, pulling out of the parking space.

Shots rang out and the car was peppered with bullets. Alex immediately felt a huge pain in his shoulder. They weren't messing around in the helicopter. Alex lost control of the car and reversed into a parked car just as further bullets ripped the tyres to shreds.

Alex climbed from the car, keeping low and using the parked cars for cover. At any moment, the car park would no doubt be swamped with armed police notified of the presence of a sniper by their colleagues in the helicopter. There were no further shots aimed in Alex's direction. Whoever was in the helicopter couldn't risk hitting the public.

Alex swore and ran for the entrance back into the shops. Alex straightened up and walked quickly to the escalator. The shoulder was painful and there was blood escaping into Alex's shirt but it wasn't visible under the jacket. Alex clamped an arm around the jacket, pushing down on the wound to try and stop the flow of blood.

Alex returned to the same shop clothes shop from earlier and without hesitation grabbed two further shirts, a red T-Shirt, jeans and a bright blue Zip Up jacket. Alex paid quickly and hurried to the shopping centre toilets.

Alex placed a thick wad of tissue against the wound and pulled on the new red T-Shirt. Alex changed into the jeans and new shirt before stuffing the suit into the waste bin. Alex left the toilets carrying the shopping bag with the spare shirt.

Several police officers and others not in uniform were rushing past Alex in the direction of the escalators. Most people were oblivious to events outside and were continuing shopping.

As Alex reached the exit there were no police challenging members of the public leaving. The police hadn't yet organised themselves and must be assuming the assassin was still inside.

Alex breathed a sigh of relief and instinctively started walking towards the station. Many people were walking or running in the same direction in panic, worried about the danger of remaining in Brighton.

CHAPTER THIRTY TWO

Powell had seen the attempted murder acted out on the giant screen. At first, people seemed not to understand what had happened but as realisation sank in, there was a general feeling of panic and people were desperately trying to get as far away from danger as possible. The police seemed unsure what to do and were overwhelmed as thousands of people ran in every direction away from the shooting.

Powell jogged towards the scene of the attack and called Jenkins mobile but received no response. Powell was fairly certain it had been Jenkins who threw himself at Bob and he needed to find out if he was okay. Bob had definitely been the target as the Prince hadn't even arrived yet. From the pictures he'd seen it was impossible to tell if Bob had been shot or just fallen under the weight of Jenkin's body.

Powell was met by a scene of complete chaos as he came close to the location of the ceremony. Most people were running in the opposite direction but a wall of police officers were stopping anyone intent on getting closer to the dignitaries. Some of the police were armed and they were all searching the crowds for any sign of a follow up attack. The police looked rightly nervous.

Powell came to the notice of one armed officer who stepped in front of him as he came close.

"Where are you going?" the officer demanded.

"I need to get to Bob Hale, the MP," Powell explained, knowing he was wasting his time. "I'm his former bodyguard."

"No one is getting past here," the officer said defiantly. "So he won't be needing any bodyguard, former or otherwise." Then in a voice that didn't invite discussion the officer said, "Please help us by moving along, Sir."

Powell hesitated but then moved a few yards away. The police officer wasn't going to allow him past no matter what he said.

Powell tried calling Jenkins again but with the same negative result. He called Bob.

"I'm surprised to hear from you," Bob answered.

"Are you okay?"

"At the moment."

"What about Jenkins?"

"He's been shot in the leg but will live."

Powell could hear the siren of an approaching ambulance. He felt a great sense of relief to hear Jenkins would live. It was Powell who had put him in danger by organising the job with Bob. If he'd been killed, Powell would never have forgiven himself.

"The police won't let me come near," Powell explained.

"Why would they? You aren't my bodyguard."

Powell ignored the cutting comment. "Why aren't they getting you away from here?"

"I'm waiting for the ambulance. Hayley thinks it's a good idea I go to the hospital with Jenkins."

Powell could see it would make a good story and engender both sympathy and votes. Bob hadn't run away from the scene but was by his injured bodyguard's side. Powell hoped he was being overly cynical. Perhaps Bob's first concern was for Jenkins' welfare.

"Will you please let me know where they take Jenkins?" Powell requested.

"I'll send you a text."

The call was already disconnected before he said, "Thanks."

Powell surveyed the area, which had become deserted except for the presence of police and reporters, who seemed oblivious to the potential danger. He decided to start walking back to his bar. There was little chance of getting a taxi in the vicinity of the town centre.

CHAPTER THIRTY THREE

Alex stared up at the station notice boards announcing all departures were delayed. Alex had to assume the police were responsible for halting any trains leaving in an attempt to trap the sniper in the town. They probably intended to check every person going through the barriers.

The concourse was packed with people desperate to find out more information and some were turning nasty, pushing people out of the way and shouting at the station staff. The way the crowd was swelling every minute, they were soon going to be packed like sardines in a tin and Alex would be unable to move. Alex didn't fancy being trapped and started to push back past the crowd, causing the hurt shoulder to complain by emitting sharp stabbing pains. It was hard work and progress was slow.

Finally, Alex made it back outside the station. It was a scene of complete chaos as an endless tide of people were moving slowly up the road from the town centre. Alex could think of only one safe place.

Alex knocked on Linda's front door, having decided not to call first so as not to give her the chance to say don't come. Alex hoped she wouldn't be with another client or out shopping, fears which were quickly allayed when Linda opened the door.

"Did you forget something?" she asked with a look of surprise.

"No but it seems I'm stuck in Brighton so I thought I would see if you are free?"

"I don't really like people just knocking on my door. You should always call first to see if I am available."

"I'm sorry but I was at the station and because of the shooting they have cancelled all the trains."

"What shooting?"

Alex was keen to get off the street. "Can I come in?"

Linda stepped back to allow Alex inside the house. "What shooting?" she repeated as she shut the front door and started upstairs.

"I don't know all the details but it's chaos out there. Don't you listen to the news?"

"Almost never. It's so depressing."

Reaching the bedroom, Linda asked, "How long do you want to stay?"

"An hour." Alex answered, actually planning to stay a lot longer but having only enough cash for one hour. Alex handed over one hundred pounds. It would buy some time and she deserved at least some payment for the inconvenience Alex was going to put her through.

"I'll be back in a minute," Linda said, quickly counting the money. "Then you can show me what you've been buying."

"Can I use the bathroom, please?" Alex asked, putting the shopping bag down.

"You know where it is." Linda left the bedroom door open as she headed downstairs.

Alex closed and locked the bathroom door, then carefully removed the jacket and shirt. The T-shirt was badly stained with blood. Alex removed the wad of tissue, which in places stuck to the skin because of the dried blood. Alex grimaced at the sight of the wound. Alex half turned around to get a better view in the mirror and was pleased to see the exit wound. Alex had been lucky but the wound needed cleaning and bandaging.

Alex washed the wound using the shirt as a cloth. It was only a temporary solution and the wound needed disinfecting. Alex realised visiting Linda wasn't such a great idea. Alex couldn't let Linda see the wounds.

"Are you okay in there?" Linda called out.

"I will just be a minute."

Alex put on the newly purchased shirt and picked up the jacket with the gun in its pocket. Alex wouldn't hurt Linda but she needed to be scared enough to do as instructed. That shouldn't be too difficult. Virtually everyone would be intimated by the threat of a gun pointed in their direction.

Alex opened the bathroom door and returned to the bedroom. Linda was wearing nothing but a smile as she lay on the bed.

"I almost started without you," Linda smiled.

"I'm sorry," Alex apologised, revealing the gun.

"I don't keep much money here," Linda said without emotion.

Alex was surprised Linda didn't seem particularly scared. "I don't want your money."

"Then what do you want?"

"I promise I won't hurt you. I just need somewhere to stay for a few hours."

"What have you done?" Linda asked suspiciously.

"I tried to shoot someone but unfortunately I missed." Alex turned on the television. "Let's see if I have made the news."

"Who did you shoot?"

"The local MP."

"Why did you shoot him?" Linda asked, moving to sit on the edge of the bed with her feet on the floor.

"It's a long story but believe me, he deserves to die."

"Can I put my robe on?"

"Of course," Alex replied, already concentrating on the television. A man was being interviewed. Alex had found the BBC news channel and immediately recognised the man being interviewed was standing on Brighton seafront.

Linda stood up and took her robe from the hook on the door. She placed her hand in the pocket of the robe and closed her hand around the alarm, she had hoped never to need to use. She held down the button for the required three seconds.

"Do you have any bandages in the house?" Alex asked.

"Are you injured?"

"It's nothing serious. Do you have any bandages?"

"No."

"Okay. I can improvise. Do you have some brandy?"

"No. Sorry."

"What about wine?"

"I always have white wine. Do you want me to fetch you some?"

Alex smiled. "Nice try but you aren't moving out of my sight. I'll come with you."

CHAPTER THIRTY FOUR

Powell had only been walking for five minutes when Afina called. He guessed she had heard the news and wanted to check he and Jenkins were okay.

"Powell, where are you?"

"I'm walking back from town." He couldn't help but notice the concern in Afina's voice.

"Mara needs help. She's pushed the panic alarm I gave her for her birthday and she's not answering her phone."

Powell was aware Afina had bought Mara an alarm. Afina was worried for her friend's safety. If a client got out of hand, Mara would push the alarm and Afina would receive a text message. Given the nature of Mara's job, she didn't want the police automatically involved. Powell had always been aware he was probably the first line of help.

"I can be there in about ten minutes," he said, already changing direction. "Perhaps she pushed the alarm by mistake."

"The button has to be held down for three seconds to avoid casual errors."

"I'll call you soon as I know something."

Powell started jogging, cursing the packed roads and impossibility of getting a taxi. He hoped there was an innocent explanation for the alarm. Perhaps Mara was with a client and had sat or lain on the alarm by mistake. She would be oblivious of the consternation she was causing and wouldn't answer her phone if she was with a client.

As he reached Mara's house, which he had only visited once for a moving in party, he stopped at the front door to draw breath and listen for any signs of trouble from inside. Mara had given him a key for use in emergencies.

He inserted the key and gently opened the door, alert to the sounds of danger. In truth, he was equally alert for the sound of two people having sex. He didn't want to disturb Mara with a client and risk giving the poor man a heart attack.

He stepped inside the hall and could hear the sound of the television from upstairs. He relaxed a little. It was the news he could hear. Not exactly what Mara and a client would be watching. He quickly checked the lounge and kitchen were empty and returned to the bottom of the stairs.

"Mara, are you here?" he called out.

There was no response. That was a little strange. Perhaps she had gone out and left the television on.

"I'm coming up," Powell announced. "Hope you are decent."

There was still no response. If she was upstairs she must have heard him call out. Unless someone was with her and stopping her from answering.

He reached the top stair and could see a couple of closed doors plus a bathroom door which wasn't closed. He headed for the room where the television was playing.

He passed the bathroom and noticed clothes in a bundle on the floor. He stepped inside to take a closer look and picked up the bundle. There was a significant amount of blood on the clothes but they were too big to be Mara's clothes. Now he was convinced Mara had intentionally pushed the alarm. He prayed it wasn't her blood on the clothes.

He slowly turned the handle of the bedroom door, uncertain what he would discover. He suspected there was no one within the bedroom. At least no one alive or he would surely have heard something by now. He pushed the door open expecting the worst but didn't step inside. He held himself sideways against the wall so as to reduce the target he was offering to anyone inside.

Alex heard the movement downstairs. Someone had entered the

124

house. Alex moved towards Mara, turned her around and put an arm around her neck, while holding the gun against her temple and indicating with a finger to the lips that she should remain quiet. Alex applied just enough pressure to Mara's neck to discourage calling out.

"Are you Mara?" Alex whispered in her ear when the man below called out.

"Yes."

"Who is he? Is he your boyfriend?"

"He is just a friend."

"Then why does he have a key to your home?"

"He is a good friend."

Alex heard the intruder announce he was coming up stairs and pulled Mara to the back of the room.

"Don't say a word," Alex warned, pressing the gun tighter against the side of Mara's head.

Even the small physical effort of holding the gun to Mara's head was hurting the shoulder. Alex hoped the gun would be sufficient deterrent to anyone about to enter the room as hand to hand combat was out of the question.

Alex listened to the man enter the bathroom. Alex regretted leaving his blood soaked clothes on the bathroom floor. Now the man would know that something was wrong. Alex listened intently but couldn't hear the man calling the police. Surely his curiosity would get the better of him and he would be concerned for his friend, who could be lying on the floor injured.

There were many possible scenarios about to unfold. The worst would be if the man about to enter the room simply turned around and fled back down the stairs. Alex would be unable to give chase if the man did flee and wouldn't shoot him in the back.

A few seconds later the bedroom door opened. Alex pointed the gun in the direction of the door.

"You!" Alex exclaimed, shocked by the appearance of the Beast's bodyguard.

Powell was focused on the gun pointed in his direction and knew he had few options. The attacker would shoot him before he was halfway across the room. At least Mara was alive. What was that show of recognition all about? Had they met before?

"Are you okay, Mara?" Powell enquired and received a positive nod in response.

"You're the last person I expected to see," Alex said.

"Do we know each other?" Powell queried, while searching his memory for answers.

"I do a good impression of a clown."

Powell was shocked. He would never have guessed it was the same person although he could now see they were similar in size.

"Do you two know each other?" Mara asked.

Powell was first to respond. "This is the person who has been trying to kill Bob Hale."

"Sit on the bed both of you," Alex instructed, letting go of Mara. "I don't want to harm either of you but I will if necessary."

Powell sat next to Mara on the bed. "What now?" he asked.

"Now we wait. What is your name?"

"Powell."

"Well Powell, how do you know Mara? Are you a customer?"

"It's complicated."

"We have plenty of time."

"She is good friends with Afina, who is the manager of my bar."

"That doesn't sound so complicated."

"Are you going to tell us your name?" Powell asked, not wanting to offer further explanation.

"It's Alex," Mara interjected.

"Where are you from?" Powell asked. He didn't recognise the accent.

"Croatia," Mara again replied.

Alex let out a small laugh. "It seems I may have been a little indiscrete with Mara."

"Why do you want to kill Bob Hale?" Powell asked. If he was going to be sat here, he intended to find out as many answers as possible.

"It is a personal matter."

"He must have done something terrible for you to be so set on revenge."

"It really is none of your business."

"I saw the clothes in the bathroom," Powell said. "Have you been shot?"

"In my left shoulder but don't get any ideas. I know you move fast but not as fast as a bullet."

"Are you going to tell us why you want to kill Bob?"

"You are his bodyguard. You must know what sort of a man he is."

"Actually I am his ex-bodyguard. I resigned."

"Really. It is a pity you were protecting him that day on the street, when I made my first attempt. Without you I would be back home now."

Powell noticed perspiration on Alex's forehead. There were also occasional grimaces revealing signs of pain.

"You need medical treatment," Powell suggested.

"We both know that isn't possible."

"I may be able to help you," Powell suggested. "I've patched up bullet wounds before."

"I am not an idiot. If I let you come near me you will try and take my weapon."

"How long are you planning to keep us here?" Mara asked impatiently.

"A few hours."

"What about my clients?" Mara asked.

"What about them? I am afraid they will have to reschedule."

"If you stay a few hours, what then?" Powell asked. "You aren't going to be in a fit state to go anywhere."

"I will be okay."

Powell didn't bother to argue. He was thinking about Afina. She would be anxiously waiting to hear news of Mara. As soon as he had the thought, his phone rang.

"I need to answer that," Powell stated.

"You can call them back later."

Powell didn't want Afina calling the police, which would be her next move if he didn't speak with her very soon. He didn't believe Alex would shoot them if they did as he asked but the arrival of the police could change everything.

"If I don't answer my phone this place will be very quickly swamped with police," Powell explained when it rang for a second time.

"What do you mean?" Alex asked concerned.

"It's a security measure we put in place some time ago. I check on Mara and if Afina doesn't hear from me then she knows there is a problem and will call the police.

"Then speak to her and tell her everything is good."

"Okay." Powell took the phone from his pocket.

"Do as I ask and no one needs to get hurt," Alex stressed.

Powell wanted to get to the bottom of Alex's story and didn't want unnecessary bloodshed. There had been more than one occasion when Alex had held back from using excessive force. Powell didn't believe Alex would kill them if they did as instructed.

Powell answered the call. "Hi Afina, everything is good. Sorry I didn't ring you straight back but it took ages to get Mara to answer the door. She'd fallen asleep on the bed and set the alarm off by mistake."

"Are you sure everything is okay?" Afina asked doubtfully. "Let me speak with Mara."

Powell passed the phone to Mara. "She doesn't believe you are okay."

"Afina, I am fine. I'm sorry but I had an early customer who had enough energy for three men and I needed to rest. I'm just going to make Powell a cup of tea. I'll call you later and we can catch up."

After a moment Mara handed the phone back to Powell and he ended the call.

"Well done," Alex said.

Mara stood up. "I might as well make that tea," she said.

"It's a good idea. We should all go down to the kitchen," Alex confirmed.

"I'm not going to run away," Mara said.

"I don't believe you would. Why aren't you more scared of me?"

"I've seen plenty of guns and I've been shot before."

"Of course, the scars. I did wonder."

"Afina and Powell saved me from some gangsters."

Alex raised eyebrows at the revelation. "You are right not to be scared, Mara. I will not hurt you. Unlike Mr. Hale, I do not believe in hurting women or children."

"You are not the typical assassin," Powell stated. "I assume it is not your normal line of work."

"You are correct. I am a soldier."

That explained a lot. Not an assassin as such but still trained to kill. "Did Bob Hale hurt someone close to you?" Powell asked.

"We will go to the kitchen and swap stories while Mara makes the tea. Please remember Powell, I do not hurt women but bodyguards are a completely different matter."

CHAPTER THIRTY FIVE

Mara made tea and they all added a dash of brandy, which she had lied about having. Alex finished his story and a silence hung over the table. Powell and Mara were both shocked by what they had heard. Mara had suffered her own abuse by her Uncle so was immediately sympathetic. As a father, Powell was close to tears when Alex retold the story of the Beast's visit to Croatia.

Powell had to admit there was something about Alex, he quite liked. This was not someone driven by money or politics. This was someone determined to gain revenge for a terrible wrong. Powell had done something similar after his daughter was murdered. He had no right to judge Alex.

"You know you shot our friend this morning," Powell said conversationally.

Mara turned to look at Powell, shocked by the revelation. "Who was shot?"

"Jenkins," Powell answered. Then quickly added, "He'll live."

"The man who dived across my target was your friend?" Alex asked.

"Jenkins is a very good friend. I recommended him to Bob Hale."

"How is he?" Alex asked, genuinely concerned.

"He is going to be okay but it means Bob will be looking for a new bodyguard."

"Where was he shot?" Mara asked.

"In the leg," Powell answered.

"High or low leg?"

"Very low."

"So he won't be out of action for long?"

"Well, he won't be running marathons any time soon."

"That wasn't the sort of action I meant."

Powell had to smile. "I'll let him know you were so concerned for his wellbeing."

"I'm glad it isn't more serious," Alex said.

"We need to get some evidence we can use against Bob," Powell suggested.

"I don't need any more evidence," Alex stated with conviction. "I want him to finally pay for his crimes. You could help me to finish the job I came here to do."

"I can't help you commit murder." Powell felt a bit of a hypocrite. He had gone to Romania and killed a man because he thought there was no other way of ensuring justice.

"I understand. This is not your problem."

"I do want to help you," Powell stressed. "I will do everything in my power to help you get justice."

"The Beast is part of your establishment. His sort always escape your type of justice. This requires my type of solution."

"We can debate this all day but right now we need to get you somewhere safe. You can stay at my place while you recover your strength."

Alex looked bewildered. "Are you serious?"

"You need help. It's not fair on Mara for you to stay here. I have plenty of room. Let me collect my car and I can drive you to my house when it's dark."

Alex laid the gun down on the table but still close to hand. "How can I trust you?"

"I don't think you have much choice. You have nowhere else to go. Or am I wrong?"

"You are not wrong but I will keep seeking revenge while there is a breath left in my body."

"You need my help."

"Then answer me one question. Why?"

"Why what?"

"Why are you willing to help me?"

"I had a daughter. The thought of someone like Bob or Street…" Powell left the sentence unfinished. "Anyway, I'd do exactly what you are doing."

"I'd cut off his cock, fry it in oil and make him eat it," Mara interjected.

Alex and Powell both turned to look at Mara.

"I believe you," Alex said.

Mara added a large measure of brandy to each of their cups. "Are you hungry? I can make some sandwiches."

"Sandwiches would be good," Alex answered. "I don't fancy anything fried."

"You're safe," Mara replied. She stood up and moved to the fridge.

"Who is this Street?" Alex asked.

"He's a famous singer and friend of Bob Hale. If Bob is still abusing children, I'll bet a penny to a pound Street is also involved."

"You know something," Alex probed.

"Bob and Street host what they call special parties."

"What makes them special?"

"I don't know."

"But you suspect something?"

Powell shrugged his shoulders. "I have no proof of anything but I would like to get an invite to one of those parties."

"Can you get an invite?"

"Probably not."

"Then help me get close to Hale and I will finish my job."

"I told you. That isn't my way."

Alex downed his brandy. "Then I will return home, recover my strength and return to finish the job at a later date."

"You aren't fit enough to go anywhere. You can stay at my house and I will find out more about Bob's parties."

"But you said you don't work for him anymore."

"True but since you shot his bodyguard I think there may be a job vacancy."

CHAPTER THIRTY SIX

Powell collected his car and drove Alex back to his home. There was a heavy presence of police on the streets but the short journey went without incident. Powell cleaned and bandaged Alex's wound before helping him to the spare bedroom.

"Get some sleep," Powell advised. "I am going to go visit Jenkins."

"The man I shot?"

"The same."

"I would ask you to wish him a speedy recovery but it may be best not to mention I am your house guest."

"I agree. There are a couple of other people I want to see so I shall be gone several hours. If you are hungry there is food in the freezer."

"Thanks. I will feel better tomorrow. Then we can talk about what we do next."

Powell ignored Alex's remark. There was no point in an argument. Powell had no doubt Alex was intent on only one objective, Bob Hale's death. Powell on the other hand was more concerned with establishing the truth and who else may be involved.

Powell drove to the hospital and noticed the town seemed to have returned to normal. In fact, the news of the shooting had probably kept people indoors and the tourists had all left town. He parked in the hospital car park and was shocked by the cost. It had become impossible to park anywhere in Brighton without it costing a small fortune.

Jenkins was philosophical about his injury. It could have been a worse result. The surgery had gone well and he was expected to make a full recovery but wouldn't be going dancing anytime soon as he was wearing a plaster cast on his lower leg.

"How are you paying for a private room?" Powell asked.

"The doctor told me Bob insisted they put me in here. He said I was a hero and deserved the best treatment possible. I like Bob. He knows what he's talking about." It was said tongue in cheek.

"He's a politician. They are very good at saying what people want to hear."

"A bit like you then."

"Have you spoken to Bob?" Powell asked.

"He phoned to check I was okay and say thanks. He asked if I could recommend anyone as my replacement."

"Did you?"

"Said I'd think about it."

"I'm going to call him shortly and offer to take my old job back."

"Why would you do that?"

"I feel a bit guilty about walking away when he needs help."

"Good thing you did or you might be lying in this bed. Even worse, given your age and the fact you're slowing down, you might now be on a slab in the morgue."

"You sound a bit off your head. It must be the drugs they've given you."

"Seriously, I'd stay away from Bob. Leave it to the police. It's not your problem."

"I feel obligated."

"I get out of here tomorrow. I don't really want to run straight back to Wales. Could you put me up at your place for a few days?"

"I think you should go home and rest up."

"I can do that at your place. If you're going to work for Bob, you won't be around much. I'd like to sink a few drinks with Afina and Mara while I have the chance."

Powell couldn't think of a good excuse for not allowing his friend to stay. He could see the suspicion growing in his friend's eyes.

"You're not telling me something," Jenkins accused. "Have you got someone living with you?"

"Not exactly but I am seeing someone."

"You've kept that very quiet."

"It's early days."

"So where did you meet?"

"None of your business."

"Sounds serious."

"Why do you say that?"

"Has she met Afina?"

"What's that got to do with anything?"

"I told you it was serious."

"Afina does not have to vet my girlfriends."

"If it wasn't serious you wouldn't be so secretive."

"I'm not being secretive."

"Then why hasn't she met Afina? You must have kept her away from the bar."

Powell knew there was a hint of truth in what Jenkins said. His emotions were always a complicated mess where Afina was concerned. She still had feelings for him and he didn't want to flaunt a new girlfriend in her face.

"Let's change the subject," Powell suggested.

"Okay. Can I just stay the one night tomorrow? Then I'll get out of your hair. That way I can have one night out with the girls before I go home."

"I have plans for tomorrow," Powell lied. "Ask Afina if you can stay at the bar."

"Won't you be staying over at Bob's?"

"Let's discuss it in the morning. And speaking of Bob I'm going to call him now and offer my services."

Bill Ward

CHAPTER THIRTY SEVEN

Powell went straight from the hospital to Bob's. Even though he was expected he had to pass strict security when he arrived at Bob's house. The police had parked directly outside and frisked him before two further officers came from within the house and escorted him back up the drive to the front door, where Hayley was waiting. They ushered him into the house, closed the front door and disappeared without saying a further word.

Hayley greeted him with a broad smile after the policemen had left. "It's good to see you, Powell."

"And you. Although I'm not sure I'm really needed. The police are obviously out in force."

"I need you," Hayley emphasised. "Quite badly actually."

Powell grinned. "That sounds good to hear but I'm not sure you need me in quite the same way as Bob."

"Definitely not. My needs require a more personal touch."

"Don't you get that from the police?" Powell teased.

"Did you see what they looked like?"

"At least the police are finally taking things seriously. They might make me redundant."

"The police haven't been much use so far," Hayley replied. "You and Jenkins have saved Bob's life, not the police. How is Jenkins?"

"He's okay. They are only keeping him in for one night."

"Good. Bob's in his study. You better go say hello. Then you can come and find me in the lounge. Don't keep me waiting too long."

Powell headed for the study, pleased that Hayley's feelings for him didn't seem to have cooled. They couldn't get up to much in the lounge but a few passionate kisses wouldn't go amiss.

Bob sat at his desk with his back to the door. The first thing Powell

136

noticed was the half empty bottle of whisky on the desk.

"How are you, Bob?" Powell asked.

"Not fucking great," Bob slurred, turning around on his chair. "This madman's never going to give up until I'm dead."

Powell hadn't heard him swear before and it seemed odd. He didn't feel inclined to offer platitudes. "I think you're right. Whoever this is has a serious personal grudge. You must have done something in your past to really piss him off."

"He's made me a prisoner in my own home."

"I think you need something to lift your spirits. Why don't you arrange to see Jack Street. Maybe have one of those famous parties you are always talking about. I'm sure Jack could arrange something to cheer you up. You can't stay trapped in your house for ever."

"The police have told me I mustn't leave the house. They say it isn't safe. Incompetent idiots! If they had caught him after the first attempts, I wouldn't be in this bloody position."

Powell refilled Bob's glass. "If you want to visit Jack Street's, I can arrange it for you as long as I come with you. The police don't need to know."

"I could do with a diversion. I'm going to go mad just staying at home."

"Let me know when and where, and I'll make the arrangements."

"I'll talk to Jack."

"Okay. Don't let anyone know about what we've discussed including Hayley. It has to remain just between us two."

"I understand. Not a word to anyone."

Powell left Bob downing another glass of whisky. He was going to have a very sore head in the morning and may not even remember their conversation but Powell felt he had planted a seed.

He found Hayley in the lounge watching the news on television.

"Anything new?" Powell enquired, sitting in an armchair.

"Nothing. Or at least the police aren't saying anything."

"They wouldn't. They aren't going to disclose anything important on television."

"So how have you been the last couple of days?" Hayley asked. "Did the police find out who was driving that van?"

"Actually they traced the van and arrested three people." He didn't want to alarm Hayley further by providing any additional detail."

"That's fantastic news. But who were they?"

"My past catching up with me. It had nothing to do with Bob."

"You must tell me all about your past one day."

"One day," Powell agreed, standing up and moving to sit next to Hayley on the sofa. "Right now though I'd rather concentrate on the present."

He leaned across and kissed her lightly on the lips. Then he kissed her again more passionately. She eagerly returned the kiss and pulled him closer. He was oblivious to his surroundings as he felt her breast. She sighed as he found her nipple with his fingers. Her hand dropped between his legs and started to massage his growing erection.

Hayley broke away breathless. She stood up and closed the door of the lounge. "The police won't come in without knocking first," she said, returning to the sofa.

"What about Bob?"

Hayley was already undoing the belt on Powell's trousers. "No arguments. I'm going to show you how much I've missed you. Consider it an early birthday present."

"It's not my birthday for nine months."

"Then consider it a belated present for your last birthday."

Hayley pushed back on Powell's chest. "Lie back and enjoy."

CHAPTER THIRTY EIGHT

Powell collected Jenkins from the hospital late morning. It was only a short journey to his house and he had a great deal to explain. Powell had decided that if he was going to be spending a significant amount of time with Bob, he actually needed someone to stay with Alex. Partly for medical reasons but also because he didn't fundamentally trust Alex not to do a runner and make another attempt on Bob's life.

Powell had questioned Alex further the previous evening to confirm there could be no doubt about Bob's guilt. After all, it had been a long time ago and Alex was just a child at the time. Memory could play funny tricks. Powell checked out the internet and indeed Bob's web site proudly spoke of his accomplishments working for the International Criminal Tribunal for the former Yugoslavia. It may not add up to much in a court of law but Powell was convinced.

Jenkins was dressed and holding onto crutches when Powell reached his room.

"Is this your lift?" a pretty nurse standing nearby asked, looking towards Powell.

"I have indeed come to relieve you of your patient. He's probably been driving you mad."

"Jenkins has been no trouble," the nurse replied. "We will miss his good humour."

"You must have kept him well sedated."

"Thanks for everything, Susie," Jenkins said. "I don't know how I'm going to get dressed by myself tomorrow."

"I'll help you," Powell suggested.

"Are you sure I can't stay another night?" Jenkins asked Susie.

"Let's get going," Powell encouraged.

Susie kissed Jenkins on the cheek and wished him well. Powell led the way to the car park. Jenkins moved surprisingly quickly with the aid of his crutches.

"I've decided you are best off staying with me after all," Powell announced on driving out of the car park.

"Your girlfriend seen sense and dumped you?"

"Not exactly. I do have someone staying with me but it's not my girlfriend."

"You're full of surprises. So you have a girlfriend and a bit on the side? What happened to the old Powell who couldn't pull a bird to save his life?"

"Was it your one track brain or your leg they operated on?"

"So it isn't someone you're shagging?"

"Alex is staying with me for a few days..." Powell hesitated but it was best just to be straight. "Alex is the person who shot you," Powell said matter-of-factly.

Jenkins turned his head sharply to stare at Powell. "Are you fucking kidding me?"

"It's complicated."

"It usually is where you're concerned. Do you seriously mean to tell me that you are hiding the man who tried to kill Bob Hale?" Then he added with a raised voice, "Not forgetting he almost killed me."

"Calm down. As I said, it's complicated. Alex has good reasons to want Bob dead."

"You've gone completely mad. I suppose you expect me to be nice to this Alex?"

"I think you should get on well. You are both soldier types. Alex is in the Croatian army."

"Well he hasn't got off to a good start with me. I don't like being shot."

"All I ask is that when we get back to my place you give Alex a chance to explain. Trust me, it's quite a story."

"Why can't you tell me?"

"It's Alex's story to tell."

"When I'm older, I'm going to write my life story but I'll have to call it fiction because the stuff you get me into sounds too unbelievable to be true."

Powell looked at his friend and smiled. "I got shot last time. It was your turn."

"Well at least it's good to hear it's your turn next."

"You're a good man," Powell said. "I don't know what I would have done without you over the last few years."

"I need a stiff drink," Jenkins replied succinctly. "And remember, I haven't agreed to anything yet."

Twenty minutes later, Jenkins hobbled into the house on the crutches. Powell took him into the lounge and fetched a large whisky from the kitchen.

"I'll be back in a minute," Powell said with a smile. He was looking forward to Jenkins meeting Alex. Sparks would definitely fly.

"Bring a refill with you."

Powell returned accompanied by Alex and a new bottle of whisky.

"Alex, this is Jenkins," Powell said.

"I'd get up," Jenkins said. "But someone shot me."

A small smile escaped Alex's lips. "I'm sorry. It was the bloody gun's fault. The scope wasn't accurate."

"Well that makes me feel much better."

"Jenkins, you said you would listen to what Alex has to say."

Alex gingerly sat on a chair opposite Jenkins.

"You been injured?" Jenkins asked.

"I was shot in the shoulder trying to escape."

Jenkins smiled. "Well that makes me feel a little better."

"I'm going to fix some food," Powell declared. "Alex, tell Jenkins your story while I'm gone."

Powell was in the kitchen when his phone rang.

"Hi Brian. You managed to track down Crawford yet?"

"Not yet but it seems he is here on official business."

"Which lunatic let him back into the country after everything he did? What will happen to his team of private contractors?"

"The two men have been charged with attempted robbery and illegal possession of a firearm."

"Robbery!"

"They confessed to wanting to rob the bar."

"What about Sam?"

"She's been charged with conspiracy to rob."

"What about attempted murder?"

"The police didn't believe there was any chance of getting a conviction. In fact, they may have a tough time proving anything against Sam. She gave a statement saying she went back to your place for a drink. She was expecting to have sex with you but you went mad and started asking crazy questions. She suggested you may have taken drugs."

"Well she obviously knew the men outside because she exchanged messages organising when they should enter the bar."

"Actually, you typed those messages. She says she had no idea what you were sending on her phone."

"The clever bitch. What about Jenkins? He witnessed everything."

"That bit of the statement makes interesting reading. She says you invited your friend over to have kinky sex and when she refused was when you turned nasty."

"Fucking hell. She should get an Oscar."

"There's more I'm afraid. When I spoke with the police off the record to support your version of events, the Chief Inspector moaned he was pissed off with interfering spooks. It turned out someone else from the service had already called him for an update on the case."

"Did he have a name?"

"Ed Manners."

"You know him?"

"Yes I know him. He's a Deputy Director like myself but his baby is counter terrorism."

"What is he like?"

"Have you heard the saying about a bull in a china shop? He's a tough bastard and very well connected in the corridors of power."

"Why do you think he was calling?"

"He was probably just doing a favour for Crawford."

"Have you asked him?"

"No. I wanted to check with you first to find out if you knew Manners."

"Never heard of him before but I already don't like him."

"It might be best we don't let him know I'm your friend. It could prove useful."

Powell thought about Brian's suggestion for a moment. "Okay. See what you can find out on the quiet. Try to find out if Manners and Crawford are old friends."

"I will and you take care. Manners is dangerous. He gets involved in the messy end of the business. He and Crawford make a particularly nasty double act."

"Thanks for the warning. Keep me informed."

Powell returned to the lounge to update Jenkins and ended up recounting the whole story of Crawford and Lara to Alex.

CHAPTER THIRTY NINE

Powell left Jenkins and Alex getting on like a house on fire. They were talking like long lost friends and sharing army stories. There was mutual respect. Powell considered his decision to get them together to be one of his better decisions. Once Jenkins heard Alex's story, he had quickly put aside any ill will for being shot. The serious leg injury became nothing more than a scratch.

Powell thought they would be good for each other's spirits as they recovered from their respective wounds. There would also be practical benefits. Alex had already volunteered to help Jenkins with getting dressed. Jenkins was checking Alex's bandages.

Powell was able to go back to work not having to worry about Alex or Jenkins. Bob had given Powell the morning off to collect Jenkins from hospital but it was time to get back to work. It was after dinner, which consisted of pizza takeaway, when Bob approached Powel.

"I thought about what you said last night," Bob said. "I'm not going to let a terrorist keep me barricaded in my house. That sort of thinking means the terrorist wins. So I spoke with Jack and he has kindly offered to organise a small party to celebrate my surviving this latest attack."

"That's the spirit. When is the party?"

"Saturday evening. It will be just a handful of trusted friends so I'll be perfectly safe."

"I'm coming with you," Powell stated firmly.

"Of course. But we don't need to take the police. In fact, it might act as a good diversion if they remain here. It will look like I am at home and they are still guarding me."

"Leave me to work out the details," Powell agreed. "Is Street okay with me accompanying you? Only he probably wasn't happy with my speaking to the police about the man I saw leaving his place, who then died."

"Jack isn't a problem. He knows you were just doing what you thought was right. The police checked out your story and you were just mistaken. The visitor you saw leaving Jack's place is still very much alive."

"That's good," Powell replied, trying to sound like he really believed it to be true. He had no doubt it was the same person but there was no point getting into an argument with Bob. Perhaps Street had friends in the police, who were covering up the truth. Powell wouldn't be surprised if that was the case. Recent experiences had made him see a conspiracy around every corner. At a later date, he would speak again to the police and convince them it was the same man.

Powell found himself looking at Bob in a different light since hearing Alex's story. Powell had to force himself to remain friendly and hide the revulsion he felt. He was pleased he wouldn't have long to keep up the charade.

Powell knew there would be no further attempts on Bob's life before the party so unlike everyone else in the house, he could relax for the next couple of days. If it turned out the party was just some old friends sharing a few drinks, he wasn't sure what he would do next. He would have to speak with Alex and come up with a new plan. Powell wasn't going to be able to just walk away from Bob's employment and forget the crimes he had committed.

Powell wondered if he should speak with Hayley about the party but decided it was too risky. She might let something slip to the police. After Saturday night, he would be direct with Hayley and ask her if she had any suspicions Bob could be abusing children. He assumed she didn't because otherwise she surely would have said something to the police. He didn't like to believe there was any other possible conclusion.

Powell was surprised late afternoon when Hayley came into the lounge in a foul mood.

"Can you believe the bloody police?" Hayley asked rhetorically. "They've halved the security team. They have other priorities and can only afford two officers."

"There have been significant cutbacks in the police budget introduced by this government."

"You can't blame the government."

"Who else should I blame?"

"I thought you said you weren't interested in politics?"

"I'm not. But if you cut budgets then there are obviously fewer people available to do the work. Bob has two officers and myself providing protection. I can see why someone would think that was sufficient."

"If the police budgets weren't cut then it would be something else. Would it be better to cut NHS budgets?"

"It would be better to make large American corporations with massive turnovers in the UK pay their fair share of taxes. Then there would be more money available for all the essential services."

"Those companies help the economy by hiring a huge number of people."

"I hire people in my bar but I still have to pay taxes. Is it any wonder the average person paying his taxes, struggling to get by, feels big business is taking the piss. And let's not mention the banks!"

"This is a new side of Powell."

"I usually keep my opinions to myself around my employers but this is a bit different. I've never worked for a politician before."

"So what's your solution?" Hayley asked.

"Outright rebellion like the French revolution. Throw all the bankers and politicians in jail and start again."

Hayley looked aghast. "Are you mad?"

"No, just enjoying winding you up. I haven't a clue about the solutions. As I previously said, I'm not into politics."

CHAPTER FORTY

When Saturday evening arrived, Powell informed the two police officers Bob had work to do in his study. He would then be going to bed early so he had given his staff the night off. Powell explained he was going out for a few beers but would be back later.

Hayley had suggested to Powell she also was free, hinting at a night out together but Powell had made an excuse about meeting up with an old friend. She had pouted but made a call and was going out with a couple of girlfriends.

The two policemen were in the kitchen when Powell stopped by to say he was leaving. Hayley had already left to prepare for her night out. While Powell distracted the policemen, Bob slipped out the front door. When Powell drove away from the house, Bob was hiding on the back seat.

Bob remained hidden until they were about a mile from his house. Powell knew with absolute certainty, the man trying to kill Bob was not lying in wait somewhere along the road but he kept up the pretence it was a possibility.

They arrived at Jack Street's house punctually at 8pm and Powell made a note there was only one car parked in front of the house, an expensive Mercedes. It obviously wasn't going to be a well-attended party. Powell committed the number plate to memory. If he didn't get introduced to the other guest, at least he might be able to trace who owned the car.

Bob led the way into the house and Jack Street told Powell some food had been put out for him in the kitchen. Powell felt a bit like servants must have felt fifty plus years earlier. He was consigned to the kitchen while the Lord of the Manor feasted with his friends.

Powell made a cup of tea and then tucked into the quality

sandwiches, which no doubt had been prepared by Sara May. She seemed to have been given the night off. Powell took that as a positive sign. The entertainment might not be suitable for her eyes. There was no rush to check what was happening in the rest of the house. There might be further guests yet to arrive.

There was a television in the kitchen, which he switched on not to watch but to give the illusion he was watching. After an hour, he opened the kitchen door and poked his head into the hallway but there was no sign of the others. He walked to the lounge and put his ear against the closed door but couldn't hear anything. It was strangely quiet for a party. He knocked on the door with his knuckles but there was no response. He opened the door and stepped inside. He glanced around the empty room. There were no signs of any partying.

Powell returned to the hall and wondered what to do next. If he looked around upstairs and was discovered, it would be hard to explain what he was doing. If the party was taking place in a bedroom then it left little doubt about the type of party.

Powell realised he hadn't properly considered the possibility Bob and Jack Street were lovers. Perhaps they and their friends were indulging their sexual tastes in adult parties. Powell wasn't bothered if they indulged in a wide range of perversions as long as it didn't involve children.

Powell was indecisive about where to go next when he heard voices coming from another part of the house he hadn't visited. The voices were getting nearer so Powell ducked back inside the kitchen. He listened from the other side of the door as two men laughed and then headed upstairs.

Powell couldn't make out what they were saying but was fairly sure one of the voices belonged to Jack Street. Powell thought about the layout of the house. When you looked at the front of the house there was a new, single storey extension on one side of the house. That was the direction from where the two men had come. Perhaps that was the party room. Hell it could be a games room with a billiard table or similar facilities. Had Jack Street taken someone upstairs for bedroom games?

Powell returned to the hall. He could hear no sound from any direction. He was going to have to venture upstairs. He tentatively climbed the stairs. The thick carpet kept the sound of his footsteps quiet. At the top he could hear no sounds coming from behind any of the ten or more doors. Were all the bloody rooms soundproofed? It was the quietest party he'd ever known.

He turned right and moved along the landing, stopping outside each door to listen but all was quiet. He retraced his steps and tried the remaining doors. At the very end of the landing he finally heard sounds from within. They were muffled but someone was definitely speaking. It was impossible to hear what they were saying but it didn't sound like two people engaged in passionate sex.

Powell questioned what he had expected to find in the first place. He supposed he hoped to discover something compellingly bad, which would force him to act. At the moment, he felt more like a peeping Tom.

He decided to return downstairs and investigate the rest of the house. He followed the hall to what he reckoned was the door to the extension. There was absolutely zero sound to be heard. Perhaps the room on the other side of the door was soundproofed. Rather than a games room it could be a form of recording studio. After all, Jack Street was a singer and extremely wealthy. He could afford to have anything he wanted in his house. A music room would be logical. But where was Bob? It hadn't been his voice Powell heard go upstairs with Jack Street.

Powell was uncertain about opening the door. He had no excuse for being in this part of the house. He noticed the sprinkler in the ceiling and wondered about calling the fire brigade. It was a ruse that had worked one time previously for Afina and helped him escape the commune. It would give him a chance to look around the house while they were distracted. It wouldn't work. Street would simply send them away.

Powell knew he had no option. Nothing ventured, nothing gained. He turned the handle and walked through the door. He found himself in another small hall with three further doors off to the side. He breathed a small sigh of relief but it was temporary. There was no going back. There were more doors to open.

His heart skipped a beat as he opened the first door and walked into a room with rows of seats in front of a large screen. It was presumably somewhere to watch films but the room was empty. He wondered what type of films Street watched?

Powell moved to the second door, which opened into another empty room with a grand piano and what looked like an impressive array of recording equipment. For a musician it was probably the equivalent of a study. Everything looked in pristine condition. It was a lot of house to keep clean.

That left only one door to open. Powell left the music room and never saw the blow coming that put him on the ground. For a second he saw a smiling face he didn't recognise, standing above him, and then he lost consciousness.

CHAPTER FORTY ONE

Powell awoke on a bed and slowly prised open his eyes. His head was pounding and he had to concentrate to remember how he came to be on the bed. How long had he been unconscious? He suspiciously looked around the room. It was an attractively furnished bedroom not a hospital room. He wasn't sure that was a good thing. It had to be one of Street's bedrooms.

His eyes came to rest on a man sitting in a chair holding a gun. He was a big man with hardly any neck but he did have a bulbous nose. He had deep lines under his eyes and a scowl on his face. He didn't look healthy and Powell would think of him as no more than another bodyguard, if it wasn't for the expensive blue suit, white shirt and red tie.

"Glad you're back with us, Powell. I was getting bored of sitting here waiting for you to wake up."

Powell realised he wasn't tied to the bed. With a shock he also realised he was totally naked and laying on top of the bed without covers. What the hell was going on!

He tried to sit up. It was a difficult process as any movement of his head compounded the pain he was feeling.

Finally in an upright position, he asked the obligatory question. "Who the fuck are you?"

"That doesn't really matter. You should be more careful creeping around someone's house. Jack has cameras in every room and I was watching you from upstairs."

"Where are my clothes?"

"They are on the floor. You can start to put them on and then we will go downstairs."

Powell was confused. His head was still groggy but something didn't add up. Had they undressed him just to search him?

He swung his legs over the side of the bed and stood up. He picked up his clothes from the floor and slowly started to get dressed. All the time, the man watched him like a hawk watching his prey. If Powell made a false move, he knew he was going to be shot. On the positive side, if they had wanted him dead, they could have ensured he never awoke.

Powell walked down the stairs with the man keeping far enough behind to be out of reach but close enough to act if necessary. He was not giving Powell any chance to strike. This was not just some celebrity friend of Bob and Jack Street. This was someone who knew what he was doing.

"We're going to the cinema," the man said over Powell's shoulder. "You know the way."

Powell remained quiet as he walked to the cinema room. He would learn soon enough what was going to happen. Once inside the room, Bob and Jack Street walked over from the other side of the room, where they had been in deep conversation.

"Take a seat," Jack Street instructed.

Powell wondered if that signalled he was in charge.

The man with the gun stayed standing to the side of Powell.

"We've had enough of your interfering in our affairs," Street continued. "The Americans weren't up to the job so we've taken out a little insurance."

Powell wasn't entirely surprised by the revelation, the attempts on his life were somehow linked to Street and his friends. The man holding the gun was almost certainly Ed Manners. He must have involved Crawford and his CIA freelancers.

Street walked to a console underneath the screen. He pressed some buttons and the screen came to life.

Powell watched an image of himself laying naked on the bed. He felt sick when a young girl who was also naked walked into the bedroom. There was a third person in the room videoing events. The girl was probably only about twelve years old and still had the body of a child. She seemed uncertain as she walked to the bed. Her eyes revealed dilated pupils and Powell was certain either voluntarily or not, she had taken drugs.

Powell could hardly watch as the girl straddled his body. The man working the video camera came up behind her and captured on film the moment he entered her tiny body but his face was hidden.

"That's enough," Powell shouted.

"But we have so much more," Street replied. "I particularly like the part where she is sitting on your face."

Powell turned away from the screen and sat staring at the man with the gun. Words would be wasted on these men. Perhaps Alex had the right idea all along. Their actions were so depraved the remedy may have to fall outside the justice system.

Street walked to the screen and turned off the recording. When he turned back, he said, "I want you to confirm to the police, you aren't sure the man you saw leaving my house was the same man who died in Brighton. We will be making an edited copy of this recording and it will clearly show you having sex with a minor. It will end up with the police if you don't do as I ask. And don't think you can try and implicate us. The police will never believe we are involved in something so heinous. We are three respected members of society while you are a nobody."

Powell took offence to being called a nobody. He now disliked Street for more than just his crap music. He was an arrogant little shit. Powell's brain was racing. The only copy of the film would still be in the house. The poor girl was also probably somewhere close to hand. He needed to act fast or both he and the girl's lives may never be the same again.

"It's a little unfair of you to take the film when I wasn't even awake to enjoy the experience," Powell complained.

Street raised his eyebrows. "Bob, it seems we may have discovered Powell's dark secret. It seems he enjoyed our film."

"I didn't see her complaining," Powell replied.

"True," Street answered. "Jasmine never complains.

"Perhaps Powell would like to star in another film before he leaves," Bob suggested.

"It would increase your insurance," Powell agreed.

"Ed, what do you think?" Street asked of the man holding the gun.

Powell turned to Ed, who Street had now unknowingly confirmed was Ed Manners. Powell remembered Brian's warning that he was an extremely dangerous man. Powell wouldn't disagree. It was undoubtedly Manners who had hit him over the head. Powell didn't think Street or Bob would have the balls for the job.

"I don't see we have much to lose by getting a better film," Manners agreed.

"I guessed your parties would be fun," Powell said. "That was why I was nosing around. I have quite varied tastes myself and it's not easy to meet other like-minded people."

"No games," Ed warned. "Not if you don't want me to hand you over to our mutual American friends. They are still very keen to get their hands on you."

"But games are exactly what I have in mind with young Jasmine," Powell replied and managed a fake smile.

"Powell has a sense of humour," Street said. "And I suspect a dirty mind. Ed, you take him back to the bedroom and I'll go fetch Jasmine. I'm quite looking forward to seeing Powell in action. It gets a bit staid always watching the same people fucking."

Powell stood up. Ed immediately took a step back and pointed his gun at Powell. He wasn't going to take any chances or be easily fooled. He wasn't an amateur like Street and Bob.

Powell wanted everything to happen slowly. He needed to waste time.

"Can I have a drink before we start?" he asked.

"What would you like?" Street asked.

"Some red wine? What about Jasmine. Does she like a drink to help get in the right mood?"

"Jasmine is much too young to drink," Street said seriously. Then he laughed out loud. "She doesn't like the taste of alcohol. She prefers coke, though not the sort that comes in a can. I gave her some ecstasy earlier so she's already in the right mood to play. I'll bring some red wine up to the bedroom."

"Thanks." Powell looked at his watch.

"We have plenty of time," Bob said with a small smile. "The police think I'm tucked up in bed."

CHAPTER FORTY TWO

Powell returned to the bedroom, closely followed by Ed Manners. The man was like a bloody shadow.

"The cameras are running and I'll be watching your every move," Ed cautioned.

"Hoping to learn a few tricks?" Powell asked.

"Girls aren't really my thing."

"You should have become a priest."

Ed smiled genuinely for the first time. "I have a friend who is a Bishop and he says the same thing."

Street entered the bedroom carrying a bottle of red wine and a glass. "I think you should like this. It's a pretty decent Claret."

"I'm sure it will be better than what I normally buy from the supermarket." Powell took hold of the glass and Street filled it half full.

Powell held the glass beneath his nose and smelt the fruity bouquet. He was no wine snob but he tasted the wine and gave an approving nod. "Excellent."

"Right, I'll go fetch Jasmine," Street said.

"Could you send her in with some clothes on?" Powell requested. "I like to slowly undress girls. It builds the excitement."

"A man who likes to take his time. A sure sign of a connoisseur whether it's girls or wine," Street answered. "The big difference between wine and girls is that wine is best when it's aged. Girls are better appreciated young."

"Very true," Powell agreed and took a further taste of his wine. "I'm guessing this is older than Jasmine? I might have to get some for my bar."

"You are quite correct," Street replied. "It's approximately twive

Jasmine's age."

"I'm going to the control room," Ed stated. "Don't take all night with the girl. Some of us have homes to go to."

Powell was left alone in the room. He hadn't bought himself much time and he would soon be joined by Jasmine. As there was no way he could keep up the pretence much longer, he urgently needed a plan B. The door had a lock but it wouldn't keep anyone at bay for any great length of time.

He sipped at the wine and placed the bottle on the bedside table. He felt like he should have asked for a large whisky. He casually walked to the window and looked out as if admiring the view. There was no obvious means of escape. If he took that route there was a better than evens chance of a leg injury and then he would be easy prey for Ed. Anyway, Powell knew he couldn't leave the house without the taped evidence of him with Jasmine.

There was a small ensuite bathroom with a lock which again would buy a little time in an emergency. He sat on the edge of the bed to wait for Jasmine. He looked again at his watch.

He didn't have long to wait. The door opened and Jasmine entered wearing a pretty, floral dress.

"Jack tells me I must be nice to you," she said.

Jasmine's presence made him feel nauseous. He felt like he'd received an electric shock to his body. He also felt a rage like almost never before. He was being watched and for both their sakes had to control his emotions.

"And I shall be nice to you," Powell replied. "Why don't you sit on the bed while I visit the bathroom."

"Would you like me to take my clothes off?"

"No!" he exclaimed. Then realised he needed to modify his reaction for those watching. "I'd like to watch you do that so wait until I return."

Powell took his time in the bathroom and didn't want to return to the bedroom but knew he had no choice.

Jasmine was sitting on the bed holding her hands in her lap. She looked anxious and tired. "You aren't going to hurt me are you? Ed always wants to hurt me."

"I'm not going to hurt you. I promise."

"Good. Jack doesn't hurt me. He's gentle. I like making Jack happy. And his friend Bob is nice."

"I promise, I won't do anything you don't want me to do."

Powell topped up his glass of wine. "Would you like something to drink?"

"I just had a drink, thanks."

Powell assumed the bedroom door wasn't locked. He had hoped to buy some time by getting a drink for Jasmine. He was soon going to have to confront Ed and the others no matter what the consequences.

The problem was he couldn't get himself killed. If he did that there would be no hope for Jasmine. Neither could recovering the film they had made be his main focus. His priority must be to get Jasmine safely out of the house, no matter the personal consequences.

CHAPTER FORTY THREE

Powell was contemplating picking Jasmine up over his shoulder and running downstairs when the bedroom door flew open. Ed and Jack entered looking flustered.

"We have visitors," Ed announced. "Jack will take Jasmine. You come with me." He pointed his weapon at Powell to suggest he wanted no argument.

Powell felt a huge sense of relief. It was the answer to his prayers.

Jack grabbed Jasmine by the arm and pulled her towards the door.

"I thought we were going to have fun," Jasmine protested.

"Later. Now you need to do exactly as I tell you," Jack said firmly as he dragged her out of the bedroom.

"Who are the visitors?" Powell asked innocently.

"Bob tells me one of them is called Jenkins. Seems he's your friend and I assume you know the other one as well."

"You aren't the only ones to want insurance. If they didn't hear from me every hour on the hour, they were to assume I was in trouble."

"Well now you are all in trouble."

"I wouldn't be too hasty if I was you," Powell warned. "They will have told another of my friends what's happening. He will be waiting to hear all is okay or he will send in the troops."

"You're bluffing."

"Your full name is Ed Manners and you work for MI5."

For the first time, Ed looked concerned. "How do you know that?"

"It's not important. My friends are going to find us shortly and they are both armed. You can try and kill us all but I don't rate your chances. Even if you succeed you will be identified as responsible."

Ed was weighing up the odds. "What do you suggest I do?"

"Get as far away from the house as quickly as possible."

"What about Jack and Bob?"

"My friends and I will also be on our way at the first opportunity."

The door handle turned and Ed instinctively reacted. His body turned towards the door and in that second Powell struck. His leg lashed out and the heel of his foot connected with Ed's kneecap, forcing it backwards in a way it was never designed to handle. Ed's knee had to support a great deal of weight. Bone cracked and cartilage tore. Ed wailed in agony as he dropped the gun and bent double in agony.

Powell didn't hesitate and delivered a second kick, this time to the groin. Ed screamed again and fell back on the floor. Powell bent to pick up the gun, confident Ed was disabled.

Jenkins hobbled into the room followed by Alex. They looked an odd couple of rescuers.

"This place has more bloody rooms than a whorehouse in Bangkok," Jenkins complained. "Seems like you don't need our help after all. Who is this?"

"Ed Manners. Look after him while I go find the others."

Powell headed for the room at the end of the landing, where he'd previously heard voices and now understood was the control room for the cameras.

Powell flung open the door but didn't immediately enter. He didn't want Bob or Street attacking him with makeshift weapons. Powell was fairly sure they weren't armed but he'd had enough blows to the head for one day.

Bob was sat watching a row of screens. He looked up and put his hands in the air when he saw Powell's gun. He looked scared, which wasn't surprising as he must have been watching on the screen what happened to Ed Manners.

"What do you want?" Bob asked.

"I want you to delete all the film for today since we entered the house. Leave no trace of us ever having been here."

Bob looked almost relieved. "Right. That seems a good idea."

"I think I'm going to deserve a bonus after today. Don't you?" Powell suggested. He was keen for Bob to think there was a simple solution to the nightmare he was experiencing.

"A bonus? Of course. A large bonus would be appropriate."

"Good. Where's Jack?"

Bob hesitated.

"Where is he?" Powell repeated.

"He's in the room."

"Which room?" Powell demanded impatiently.

"He has a special panic room in his bedroom."

"You better show me."

Powell followed Bob to the room next door, which had a huge double bed and expensive furnishings. Along one side of the room were mirrored wardrobes.

"Where is it?" Powell asked.

Bob walked to one of the wardrobes and opened it to reveal a normal hanging rail with clothes. He pushed the clothes aside and pointed to the back of the wardrobe. "He's in there."

Powell looked inside but couldn't see anything except a wardrobe. "How is it opened?"

"No idea. He showed me the inside once but not how it's opened."

"Can he see and hear us?" Powell asked.

"Yes. He has the same camera access as in the other room."

Powell stood in the centre of the room. "Jack, I want you to send the girl out. I'm not interested in you. I just want Jasmine. If not I'm going to pull this place apart until I have enough evidence to destroy your career and life. If that doesn't work, I will call the police. I'm not leaving here without the girl." He paused to allow his words to sink in. "If you send her out, we will leave and I hope we never get to meet again. I'm going to go wait outside now with Bob. Send the girl out."

Powell nodded at Bob to follow him and left the bedroom. He led the way back to the other room with the cameras. Once inside he instructed Bob, "Show me Jack's bedroom."

Bob sat and quickly brought up an image of the bedroom where they had been a couple of minutes earlier. After a minute, during which time Jack had no doubt been considering his options, Jasmine emerged from the wardrobe.

Powell hurried back to the bedroom and found Jasmine sitting on the bed.

Her eyes lit up when she saw Powell. "Hello again. Are we going to play now?"

"Not right now, Jasmine. Come with me." He took her hand and led her back to the bedroom where Ed was being held.

"I don't want to play with all of you," she said, obviously reluctant to enter the bedroom when she saw the three men.

"Don't worry," Powell reassured her. "These are my friends and we're here to help you."

She was staring at Ed who was in agony on the floor. "What happened to him?"

"He hurt himself," Powell answered.

"Like fuck I did," Ed interjected angrily. His face was contorted in pain. "I need a doctor."

"Keep quiet," Jenkins commanded. "Otherwise I'll break your other leg."

"He didn't hurt himself. Did he?" Jasmine asked.

"Not exactly," Powell replied.

Was it you who hurt him?"

"Yes."

"Good," Jasmine said and being careful to keep well away from Ed, went and sat on the bed.

"Who is this girl?" Alex asked.

"This is Jasmine. We are going to get her away from here."

"Did they…?" the question by Alex went unfinished.

Powell gave a slight nod of his head.

Alex walked across to Jasmine. "Hello Jasmine. My name is Alex. I promise these men won't hurt you anymore."

"Hello Alex." Jasmine's face lit up in a smile. "I like you."

Alex turned back and stared at Ed. Powell thought of the saying, *if looks could kill.* Ed avoided Alex's gaze and stared down at the floor.

"Where's Jack Street?" Jenkins asked. "I think I'd like to spend some time alone with him."

"He's locked himself inside a panic room in his bedroom. There's no way to get him out."

"What about if we threaten to cut up his friend here?" Jenkins stared at Ed, who turned an even whiter shade of pale.

"If I thought it would work I'd be the first in line to use the knife," Powell replied. "But Street's an odious little shit, who I'm sure won't come out of his bolt hole no matter what we do."

"It might still be worth a try," Jenkins said, smiling at Ed.

"Feel free if he causes any trouble."

Alex held up a large serrated edged knife. "I don't think this man will cause us any trouble."

Powell smiled inwardly. He was sure Ed would be terrified and cause no problems. "Please look after Jasmine for me," he requested.

Jenkins hobbled closer to Powell and whispered, "Do you know what she's taken?"

"Ecstasy, I suspect. I haven't seen any signs of needle marks on her arms. They would find it easier to get her to take a pill. Street said she also likes cocaine."

"Street and his friends have a lot to answer for."

"That is why we are here."

"This is all getting very messy," Jenkins said." We could be getting into a heap of trouble with the police. Not to mention MI5. Killing them all and burning the house down might be the best way to proceed."

"I know what you mean but that could bite us on the arse just as easily. We have to find another way. Right now I have to go do something about the cameras. I'll be as quick as I can."

Powell returned to where he had left Bob. "Do you know how this system works?"

"More or less."

"It seems to use videos to record images. Isn't that old fashioned? Why doesn't Street use a digital system?"

"Digital systems rely on wireless connections to a PC," Bob explained as if he was talking to an idiot.

"I still don't get it."

"If it's wireless, anyone within a reasonable range would be able to view the images. That doesn't make sense for someone as famous as Jack."

"Especially given what Jack liked to record."

Bob said nothing.

"So there isn't a backup anywhere?"

"Are you kidding?"

Powell realised it was a stupid question. Street wouldn't want more than one copy and certainly none kept anywhere except at the house.

"Have you collected up all of today's videos yet?" Powell continued.

"Yes, I've four here and there's the fifth one downstairs in the cinema room." For a man used to being in charge, Bob had become very subservient.

"It's almost time to be on our way." Powell said, taking hold of the videos. "Where is the current video kept?"

"Here," Bob answered, pointing.

"Take it out." Powell was no expert but reckoned without a video in the machine nothing further could be recorded.

Powell was also assuming Street had a live feed of the cameras from the panic room, to spy on what was happening in each room, but no means of recording events. It was more assumptions than he liked but the bottom line was, Jack Street wasn't going to be calling the police to report a crime anytime soon, not without having a huge amount of explaining to do.

"Where does Jack keep his old recordings?" Powell asked. He wanted some evidence of previous abuse on the part of Jack and his friends.

"I think he has a safe somewhere in his bedroom."

Powell recognised that was probably a dead end. They had no way of breaking into a safe and no way of persuading Jack to open it. He hoped the current day's tapes might have the evidence he needed.

Powell was trying to cover all possible scenarios but there was one which still caused him particular concern.

CHAPTER FORTY FOUR

Powell left Bob behind and returned to the bedroom. He was confident Bob wouldn't run away or call the police. He thought Powell was going to take him back home and then expect to receive a large bonus. Powell laid the videos on the bed, took a pillowcase from one of the pillows and then placed the videos inside the pillowcase, to make them easier to carry.

"Time to be going," Powell announced.

"I need an ambulance," Ed pleaded.

"I'm sure your friend Jack will come out of hiding and call one for you, once we've left." Powell had no sympathy for Ed's condition. In fact, he hoped it hurt like hell. Ed Manners was a monster. "Give me your phone. I don't want you calling your American friends the moment we leave the room."

Manners reluctantly handed over his phone.

"Where are we going?" Jasmine asked.

"Back to my place."

"Did Jack say that was okay?"

"We don't need to ask Jack. You will be safe with us."

Jasmine seemed uncertain. "Jack looks after me."

"He hasn't been doing a good job of looking after you, Jasmine. He allowed Ed to hurt you."

"That wasn't Jack's fault."

"We'll talk about Jack later," Powell replied gently. He didn't want an argument with Jasmine. She was going to need a huge amount of psychological help from experts and he doubted she would ever truly recover from her ordeal.

Powell was holding the pillowcase full of videos. He held out his spare hand to Jasmine. "Let's go," he said and she took his hand.

"I'm not ready to leave yet," Alex declared, pointing a gun at Powell.

"What the fuck you doing?" Jenkins demanded.

"I'm sorry. Just take the girl and go."

It was the scenario that had caused Powell concern. "We all need to leave together."

"My work here isn't finished. Where is he?"

"I told you. Street is hiding in the panic room."

"Where is the Beast hiding?"

"I need to deliver him back to his house," Powell insisted. "Otherwise, if anything happens to him, I will be the prime suspect."

"Powell, I am grateful to you and your friends but make no mistake, you do not want to come between me and the Beast. You are wasting time. Take the girl and go."

"I don't believe you will kill me or Jenkins for that matter," Powell said without complete conviction.

"It will not be necessary to kill you. I have only to put a bullet in your leg and that will be the end of the argument. It seems stupid to take a bullet for no reason."

"Let's just go," Jenkins encouraged. "I would do the same in Alex's position."

"Jenkins is right. You should just go. Jasmine needs your help."

Powell wasn't in a position to argue. He looked at Jasmine's young face and thought of the innocence the men had destroyed. She was the one deserving of his sympathy.

"Jenkins, give Alex your car keys. We can take mine."

Jenkins took the keys from his pocket and threw them on the middle of the bed. "Good luck," he said and hobbled to the door.

"He's in the end bedroom on the left," Powell said and still holding Jasmine's hand, followed Jenkins out of the room.

CHAPTER FORTY FIVE

After a moment, Alex followed Powell out of the bedroom. The others had reached the bottom of the stairs. A door at the end of the landing was thrown open and Bob Hart emerged from one of the rooms.

"What's going on?" Bob asked to no one in particular.

"We meet at last," Alex answered and advanced along the landing, barely able to believe finally being face to face with the Beast.

"Who are you?"

"A friend of Powell. I was just coming to get you."

"Are we leaving?"

Alex was standing in front of Bob. "Don't you recognise me?"

"Have we met before?"

"Many years ago but more recently we met on the pavement outside your office. Unfortunately, Powell stopped me from putting an end to your miserable life."

Bob's face turned to a look of horror at the realisation of who he was confronting. "Please don't kill me," he begged. "I'm a wealthy man. I can give you money. I agreed to pay Powell a large bonus."

"People like you think everything has a price. Some things can't be bought."

"I'll do anything you want," Bob pleaded. "Please don't hurt me."

"You disgust me. You have no morals."

Alex opened the nearest door and seeing it was a bedroom, indicated with the gun for Bob to enter. Bob was either unable or unwilling to move so Alex thrust the barrel of the gun into Bob's ribs.

"If you don't move, I will shoot you right here," Alex stated and gave Bob a push towards the bedroom. "It's your choice."

Bob did as instructed and led the way into the bedroom.

"Sit on the bed," Alex ordered. "Is this Street's bedroom?" Alex had noticed the grandeur of the room.

"Yes."

Alex had an idea and decided to search the room, starting with the bedside tables and immediately hit the jackpot. There were enough supplies to fill a shelf in a pharmacy. There were plastic bags containing white tablets, which at a guess were probably ecstasy tablets not sleeping pills. There were also bags of white powder, which it was easy to imagine were cocaine.

Alex found a large brown slab, which was recognisable as heroin. There were hypodermic needles, a spoon, a lighter, cotton balls and a rubber band. Alex knew this amounted to everything needed to inject heroin. Alex had experimented a little as a teenager but it had offered only a temporary escape from the nightmares. Army training and service had provided the long term solution .

Alex had his back to Bob and didn't immediately reveal what was in the drawer. Perhaps he knew anyway. It was appropriate Bob should die as the result of drugs rather than a knife, which had been the original intention. Seeing the state of Jasmine had prompted the idea. The cause of death might even be accepted as an accidental drug overdose. That might make life easier for Powell.

"Lie on the bed on your front and put your hands behind your back," Alex instructed.

Bob did as he was told without argument.

Alex opened a couple of the mirrored wardrobes and found a collection of ties on a special hanger. Alex took down two, which were made of silk and would be perfect for the job.

"I can give you names," Bob suddenly said.

"What names?"

"I know many important people who share my weakness for young girls."

"You mean children?" Alex wanted to hear the Beast admit to his perversion.

"Yes."

Alex moved to the bed and firmly tied Bob's hands and then his feet. He positioned Bob's head looking away from the mirror.

"Don't move a muscle," Alex ordered. "I've decided not to cut off your cock and leave it in your mouth but don't push your luck. There is still time for me to change my mind again."

Alex was thinking about Bob's willingness to trade names for his life. Powell could be trusted to pursue justice against the other names.

"Tell me some names," Alex demanded.

"Get me out of here and I'll give you the names," Bob replied.

"I'm not stupid," Alex answered angrily. "You give me the names now."

"Only when you deliver me back home."

Alex decided it was a waste of time. Every minute spent in the house, increased the chance of being caught. Alex was never going to allow the Beast to leave this house alive.

Alex noticed the growing dampness on the bed around Bob's middle. He was pissing himself and Alex was pleased. Anything that increased his discomfort was to be applauded.

Alex returned to the bedside drawer and removed the heroin, spoon and lighter. Alex was no expert but couldn't really get it wrong, given exact amounts weren't important. Alex put some of the tar on the metal spoon, then added a few drops of water from the bottle beside the bed. Finally, Alex heated the mixture by putting the lighter under the spoon. After a short time the tar combined with the water into one consistency.

Alex sucked the heroin into the syringe, then squirted out a bit to get any air bubbles out of the syringe. The Beast wasn't going to die quickly from an air bubble accidentally injected into his blood stream.

Alex sat on the bed and took hold of Bob's arm, then tied the rubber band around the upper arm so as to find a vein.

"What are you doing?" Bob screamed as he felt the band pulled tight.

"Shut the fuck up or I will change my mind about cutting you. I'm just going to put you to sleep while I make my getaway. I don't want you calling the police the second I leave the house." It was an illogical reason given Jack Street's presence but Bob wasn't thinking logically.

Alex injected a quarter of the contents of the syringe into Bob's vein. Bob didn't move or react, just let out what sounded like a pleasurable moan.

"Before I leave, I want you to know who I am. You must be wondering why I want you dead? We've met before."

Despite the drugs, Bob's mind was still coherent. "We have? When?"

"You came to my home in Croatia many years ago. My name is Alex."

"You're mistaken. I don't know any Alex. I've never met anyone called Alex."

"You brought a Barbie doll with you."

Bob thought for a moment, dragging a memory from the recess of his brain. "The girl was called Mia not Alex."

"My father named me Aleksandra but my mother always preferred to call me by my middle name, which was Mia. When I joined the army I chose to be called Alex."

"Mia. You are the beautiful little Mia?"

"Yes. It was me you abused. You are responsible for my nightmares and my brother's death."

"I never touched your brother."

"Not directly but indirectly you killed Luka. He blamed himself for not protecting me. He turned to drugs and killed himself."

"You can't blame me…"

"Be quiet," Alex demanded. "You are responsible. How many other lives have you ruined?" Tears were escaping from the sides of her eyes. "I was just eleven years old. Did you feel no guilt as you forced your adult cock inside my child's body?"

"I paid a lot of money. Blame your mother not me."

"I do blame her and maybe her crime is even worse but it was one time. You are still destroying young lives. I have met Jasmine. How many others have there been over the years? You have to be stopped."

"You said you weren't going to kill me," Bob said, suddenly worried.

"I lied. Just like you did when you said it wouldn't hurt very much."

"I can't help myself," Bob screamed.

"You made choices. We live and die by our choices. I learned that in the army."

Alex plunged the remainder of the syringe into the Beast's arm and he quickly fell silent. Alex checked his breathing and it was shallow. He seemed like he was in a deep sleep. Soon to be a permanent sleep, Alex anticipated.

Alex undid Bob's hands and massaged his wrists a little to get rid of the signs of having been tied up and then did the same with his legs. Then Alex turned him on his front. The overdose story looked believable.

As Alex looked down at the man she had thought about every day for so many years, her thoughts turned to her young brother. There was no feeling of elation. She had done what was necessary. She needed to get on with her life and return to Croatia.

CHAPTER FORTY SIX

Powell took Jenkins and Jasmine back to the bar. He had told the police officers at Bob's house, he was going out for a few drinks. Jenkins was his alibi and the bar an obvious location for their drinking. Powell had to assume Alex would by now have killed Bob and come the morning, if not sooner, the shit would hit the fan when the police discovered Bob wasn't at home.

Powell's instinct was to take Jasmine to the nearest hospital but that would lead to questions he couldn't easily answer. Certainly not without ending up in a police cell. If she had taken ecstasy she would wake up feeling rubbish but otherwise physically okay. He hoped she wasn't addicted to cocaine, which would lead to withdrawal symptoms that required medical assistance.

Powell had called Afina upstairs and explained Jasmine had been abused and needed help. Afina wasted no time with questions but set about helping Jasmine into bed. They forced her to drink a large glass of water so she didn't become too dehydrated but she had refused food.

Powell informed Afina, he and Jenkins had spent the evening upstairs drinking. Jenkins leg made it impossible to go out to a crowded bar. Powell knew if anyone should enquire about his whereabouts, such as the police, she wouldn't hesitate to back up his alibi, despite knowing it was a lie.

Powell needed to discover more about Jasmine. Where was her family? How did she come to be at Jack Street's house? Somewhere there must be parents, who presumably had no idea of their daughter's behaviour. It was possible she had run away from home. Brian would be able to search the police database of missing children.

Powell didn't feel he owed any great duty to the parents. He may be proved wrong but he thought they had been negligent in their duty of acre towards their daughter. He decided to wait until morning before making final decisions about her welfare. Jasmine had been too tired and full of drugs to answer any questions before going to bed.

Once Jasmine was in bed, Powell called Brian and updated him on events, especially Ed Manners. Powell had been unable to check the content on the videos as he didn't have a video player. They might contain damning evidence against Manners and the others but it would be the morning before that was revealed. Brian was reluctant to go to the Director General without concrete evidence. Manners was known to have friends in high places.

Powell asked Brian if there was any update on Crawford. Brian had hit a brick wall. Crawford had disappeared but was believed to still be in the UK. The Americans refused to believe he was involved in any action against Powell. He was tracking down a terrorist.

What the Americans truly believed was irrelevant. They were not willing to help and had issued a strong warning not to interfere with Crawford's work. Powell told Brian not to worry. Powell had more immediate issues requiring his attention.

Powell and Jenkins had a large whisky while they sat and discussed the evening. They decided not to call Alex. If she was arrested, they didn't want any phone calls traced back to them. They turned on the television to keep track of the news.

"I need to say thanks," Powell said.

"Always a pleasure," Jenkins replied. "Especially when it involves helping someone like Jasmine. Alex had the right idea. We should have killed them all."

"Alex is very special."

"She deserves a decent life after everything she's gone through," Jenkins said. "When you first brought her into the lounge, I was shocked. I'd expected Alex to be a man. Her story was horrifying."

"Very true and sadly child abuse doesn't seem to be rare. Even footballers are now coming out and recounting stories of abuse."

"You know, she and I have something in common."

"You mean apart from the army?"

"We both fancy the hell out of Mara."

"You should tell Mara how you feel," Powell suggested.

"Can't do that. She's not the sort to settle down with one man and I'm too old fashioned to want any other type of relationship."

"You surprise me sometimes with your insights," Powell said. "You know if she ever does settle down with one person, it's more likely to be with a woman than a man."

"I know," Jenkins answered, obviously resigned to the fact.

"It is unfortunate we couldn't get to Jack Street," Powell said, intentionally changing the subject.

"He can't stay hidden away for ever."

"We're not vigilantes."

"I guess not but the rich and powerful do seem able to avoid justice too often."

Powell also believed that to be the case. "Let's hope the tapes have some evidence we can provide to the police."

"We've broken a fair few laws tonight," Jenkins said with a smile. "What do you think Jack Street will do?"

"Your guess is as good as mine. I don't believe he will rush to involve the police. He might well look to Ed Manners to clear up the mess. It's more in his line of business."

"What are we going to do?"

"If the tapes have evidence of Street and Manners abusing Jasmine we could make sure a copy falls into the hands of the police."

"And if they don't?" Jenkins asked.

"I'm not sure. With the tapes and a statement from Jasmine that might be enough to push them to plead guilty and put them in jail for many years. Without the tapes, I don't know if Jasmine will be up to a prosecution and all that entails. We need to get in touch with her parents."

"I'd be interested to know how their daughter ended up at Street's place." There was disgust in Jenkins' voice. "I'm sure he didn't kidnap her. It's bloody criminal."

"There could be many innocent explanations."

"Well it can't be because she was a fan of his music," Jenkins joked.

Powell's phone rang. He looked at the number, which was a landline he didn't recognise and answered with a cautious, "Hello."

"It's me," Alex said. "I only have a minute. Tell Jenkins to collect his car from the Gatwick Hilton. The keys are on the front tyre on the driver's side. It's in Bay 312."

"Did everything go as you planned?"

"Yes. Thanks for all your help. Please also be sure to thank Mara."

"I will. When is your flight?"

"I am on the first flight out in the morning. I guess I will read in the press what happens to the others. I hope they get what they deserve."

"I promise they won't get away with what they have done to Jasmine and probably many others."

"I believe you. Hale suggested there were many other important figures, who shared his interest in children. If you or Jenkins ever want a holiday, come and visit me in Croatia. It's a beautiful country. Tell Jenkins I hope his leg recovers soon."

It was the first time Powell had heard Alex call Bob by his name. She had always previously referred to him as the Beast. Powell hoped it was a small sign she was exorcising her demons.

"Good luck," Powell replied. "I will make a point of visiting Croatia in the future."

"Thanks for everything," Alex said and ended the call.

CHAPTER FORTY SEVEN

Powell arrived at Bob's house promptly at 8.00am. Afina was looking after Jasmine and Jenkins was scouring the internet looking for a video player.

Powell found the police were drinking coffee in the kitchen. Hayley hadn't yet arrived.

"Good night?" the senior policeman called Glen queried.

"Yes but I'm paying for it now."

"There's coffee in the pot."

"Thanks." Powell helped himself to a mug of coffee. "Anything interesting to report ?"

"Been very quiet all night with you and Hayley out."

"Is Bob up yet?" Powell asked.

"Don't think so. He usually comes down here for coffee soon as he wakes. That is, when Hayley isn't around to get it for him."

The second policeman called Ian spoke. "I wouldn't mind a Hayley, running around doing everything for me."

"I don't think Mandy would approve," Glen said. "And she doesn't provide Bob with everything you get from Mandy."

"I've been doing so many night shifts recently, I'm beginning to forget what Mandy even looks like. She's leaving for work as I get home."

Powell took his coffee and walked to the lounge, where he turned on the news. There was still no mention of Bob, which wasn't surprising. The policemen in the kitchen would hear the news before it was broadcast on television. He watched for twenty minutes before he heard Hayley arrive.

He heard her go to the kitchen and a few minutes later she walked upstairs, probably taking Bob his coffee. He prepared himself for the inevitable fallout. After a minute, he heard Hayley rushing down the stairs. She ran into the lounge.

"Where the hell is Bob?"

"Isn't he upstairs?" Powell answered.

"No he bloody isn't."

"Are you sure?"

"Yes I'm sure. And he's not answering his phone."

"Let's check with Glen." Powell said, already striding towards the kitchen.

Glen looked up from his coffee expectantly. "Something wrong?"

"Hayley says Bob isn't upstairs."

Glen jumped up from his chair. "Ian, go check upstairs," he commanded. "Where the fuck is he?" he asked turning back to Powell and Hayley.

"No idea," Powell replied. "When did you last see him?"

Glen thought for a moment. "I didn't see him after you two left last night."

"Well he can't have been abducted," Powell said. "Not from under your noses. He must have voluntarily gone out somewhere. Perhaps that's why he gave us the night off."

"Where would he go?" Glen asked.

Hayley was on her phone but getting no response.

"No idea," Powell responded. "He does have a way of escaping out his window. He did that to avoid the attack by the clown."

Ian came back into the room. "He's not upstairs," he confirmed.

"Wait here a minute," Glen instructed and rushed out of the room.

Ian looked worried. "Is there nowhere you can think of he might have gone?"

"Perhaps he paid a visit to Jack Street?" Powell suggested, looking at Hayley.

"I'll call him," Hayley responded.

Glen walked back in. "His car is still here. It doesn't make any sense."

"I'm not getting any answer from Jack Street," Hayley announced.

"How would he get there without his car?" Glen queried.

"I suppose Street could have picked him up. Perhaps Bob sneaked out and met Street."

"Why would he do that without telling anyone?" Hayley asked.

"Perhaps Street was organising some special entertainment. The sort Bob wouldn't want anyone to know about."

"What do you mean?" Glen probed. "What sort of special entertainment."

"Powell, can I please have a word with you in the lounge," Hayley demanded.

"You better call your superiors," Powell said to Glen.

Glen nodded and Powell followed Hayley to the lounge.

"What the hell do you think you're doing?" Haley asked, once they were in the lounge with the door firmly closed.

"What do you mean?" Powell replied.

"What were you insinuating in there?"

"Come on Hayley, you've worked for Bob for a long time. Don't you ever ask yourself what goes on during these party evenings with Jack Street and friends."

"It's none of my business," Hayley responded defensively. "And it's definitely not the business of a bodyguard."

"Street is accused of being a paedophile. Open your eyes."

"We can't have that sort of scandal. It would ruin Bob's career."

"And yours?"

"Bob's a good man," Hayley replied, ignoring Powell's barbed comment. "He could be our next Prime Minister. We need to avoid a scandal at any cost. You mustn't make accusations that could damage his reputation."

"Are you telling me you don't mind if the next Prime Minister associates with a paedophile who abuses children?"

"You have no proof Jack is a paedophile."

"And what about Bob? Answer me honestly, Hayley. Would you swear Bob has never touched a child?"

"Bob's not like that but even if he is it's none of your business."

"Are you mad. It's the business of all decent people to root out anyone who abuses children. If you have ever had even the slightest suspicion Bob is a paedophile, you should have gone straight to the police and to hell with your career."

Powell had heard enough. He didn't want to hear Hayley defending herself. He knew there could be no future for the two of them. He couldn't spend time with someone who put career before the abuse of children. He turned and walked back to the kitchen.

CHAPTER FORTY EIGHT

Powell had little to contribute to the police enquiry. He was at a loss to explain what had happened to Bob. There was general consensus Bob must have left the house of his own free will. The reason was a complete mystery. After an hour, Powell was allowed to return home. He wasn't suspected of any crime and the police were well aware he had previously saved Bob's life.

When Powell arrived back at the bar, he was met by Jenkins coming out of the office.

"How's Jasmine?" Powell asked.

"She seems confused and doesn't understand who we are or why she is here, which is hardly surprising. Afina is upstairs trying to provide some answers."

"What about the videos?"

"I just returned from town with a cheap video recorder. I've set it up in your office. We can watch the videos soon as you're ready. I didn't fancy watching them by myself."

"Good. Let me just go check on Afina, first."

Powell went upstairs to the lounge and found Jasmine sitting on the sofa with Afina.

"Hi Jasmine, do you remember me?"

She looked completely different to the previous night. Her eye makeup was smudged and she looked like she hadn't slept. She was wearing the t-shirt Afina had provided to wear in bed and she looked her young age.

"I think I remember you," Jasmine replied uncertainly.

"I need to borrow Afina for a minute. Have you had breakfast?"

"I'm not really hungry."

"You can have anything you want. We do a great pancakes with maple syrup."

"Can I have ice cream with it?"

"Like I said, anything you want," Powell encouraged. "What flavour?"

"I love chocolate chip."

"Coming right up."

Powell's thoughts turned to his daughter. It had been Bella's favourite ice cream flavour. She'd once slept in the same bed as Jasmine had spent the night. Bella had been murdered, which left him devastated but he was thankful she had never been abused like Jasmine. It was impossible to comprehend why anyone would abuse an innocent child.

"Why don't you get dressed while I go talk to Powell and get breakfast organised," Afina suggested.

Powell waited until he was downstairs before speaking to Afina. "Let's go in the office," he said.

Jenkins was sat behind the desk.

"How is she?" Powell asked, perching on the corner of the desk.

"Confused," Afina replied. "She doesn't remember too many details about yesterday. She wanted to know when she could go back to Jack Street's."

"You have to be kidding?" Jenkins asked, shocked.

"She says Jack Street looks after her. She doesn't mind doing things for him that make him happy."

Powell suppressed the revulsion he was feeling. "What about her parents?"

"She doesn't have any. She lives in a care home. She says Jack Street is a regular visitor and recently she's been spending more and more time at his place. She actually seems to like him."

Everyone seemed lost for words.

"Poor kid," Jenkins said, breaking the silence. "What are we going to do?"

"Afina's going to make her some breakfast. We'll take a look at the videos and then decide on the next steps. By the way, did you ask how old she is?"

"She's twelve. She says Jack Street bought her loads of presents for her birthday. Then a few weeks later it was his birthday. She felt guilty she hadn't bought him a present and he suggested there was a way she could make him happy. That was about three months ago."

"The bastard has to pay for what he's done to her," Jenkins said adamantly.

"We need to check the videos. Afina, can you please get Jasmine's pancakes."

Powell waited for Afina to leave the office before he turned to look at the television screen. He didn't want Afina to be subjected to watching Jasmine being abused. She had personally suffered too much abuse in her own life.

Afina was a remarkable young woman. She was one hundred per cent reliable in every situation. It didn't matter what you threw at her, she would deal with it and never complain. She was very different to Hayley, who was driven by personal ambition. Powell wondered if he was looking for love in all the wrong places. The answer may lay closer to home.

CHAPTER FORTY NINE

The videos were difficult to watch. Both Powell and Jenkins had seen more than their fair share of death up close but that paled in comparison with watching the destruction of a young child's innocence. The tape from the afternoon revealed Jack Street having sex with Jasmine and provided all the evidence Powell had hoped for to be able to expose Street.

The only tape showing Ed Manners having sex with Jasmine was the one Powell had already seen, which included himself. Powell burned the tape in a sink and washed the remnants down the drain. He still had to decide the best way of using the tape of Street. If he passed it to the police, they would want to find the girl featured in the tape. That in turn would inevitably lead to Jasmine. Was it best for her to be dragged into a court case? Powell wondered if he was concerned for Jasmine or the fact once they found Jasmine, he might be implicated.

Bob's body was found at the bottom of Beachy Head, one of the most notorious suicide spots in the country. Powell received a call from a distraught Hayley, informing him of the news mid-morning. She confirmed Powell's misgivings by seeming more concerned about the impact on her future than Bob's actual death. Powell showed no sympathy. He advised her to take a holiday and then look for a new job.

An autopsy would reveal the drugs in Bob's system and Powell thought it the clever work of Ed Manners to stage the suicide. It was a plausible scenario. Bob was depressed and under the influence of the heroin had jumped from the top of the cliffs. There was nothing to implicate Street or Manners.

A phone call to Brian revealed Ed Manners had informed the

Director General he had slipped and fallen downstairs. He would be taking a few days off work. Powell asked Brian to say nothing about what they had discovered. Brian had no news about Crawford. The man was as slippery as an eel.

Afina had provided Jasmine with breakfast and then invited Mara to the bar so she could share her own story of being abused by her Uncle. Between Afina and Mara, they managed to befriend Jasmine and show how Jack Street was simply a sexual predator, who did not deserve Jasmine's affection. The difficulty was that Jack Street offered something better than the life she had experienced in the care home. Afina and Mara promised they would stay in touch with Jasmine and she could visit them both on a regular basis.

By the afternoon, Jasmine had shown her resilience and was enjoying a Burger meal with a huge pile of chips. She had definitely taken to Afina. She was impressed Powell owned a bar and he promised she could eat there any time she wanted.

Powell could no longer put off returning her to the home. He asked Afina to make an appointment with the man in charge of the care home, which was located in Patcham, on the edge of Brighton. Jasmine's memory of specific events was unreliable and she agreed to tell the head of the care home she had run away from Street and Afina had found her on Brighton beach, hungry and tired.

When, in a few days, the tape officially surfaced and she was questioned by police, she would tell them about what went on at Street's house but details would inevitably be hazy as he always provided happy pills to put her in the mood. Afina had stressed she shouldn't mention Powell.

What Street's reaction would be to being arrested was difficult to predict. Powell couldn't imagine Street would want the glare of publicity that would come with a public trial. The police might try and offer a deal for information about other paedophiles but he surely wouldn't want to turn against the very dangerous Manners.

Afina returned Jasmine to the care home. Powell drove and sat outside the very large Victorian house while Afina took Jasmine inside.

"How was it?" Powell asked when Afina returned to the car.

"The manager is a Mr. Sharpe. He was shocked she had run away from Street. He kept going on about how Street was such a charming and helpful man. How he bought everyone in the home Christmas presents. I told him, I thought she had been mistreated by Street but I didn't have any proof."

"What did he say to that?"

"I think he was genuinely concerned but he was also worried about losing his job. I made him promise Jasmine wouldn't be allowed anywhere near Street."

"Do you trust him to keep his word?" Powell queried.

"Yes. He was definitely scared when I said I would go to the papers and the police, if I ever heard of any other child in his care not being properly looked after."

"Good. I don't entirely blame the man. Street has been fooling a great many people for a very long time. When the tape comes out and Street is shown to be a paedophile, Jasmine will get the professional help she needs."

"I feel so sorry for Jasmine."

"How was she when you took her inside?"

"She was fine on the surface. She went off to play with some friends."

"And you told Sharpe, you would like to keep in contact with Jasmine?"

"He said that was okay but they would have to run some police checks. I think he called it a CRB check. He gave me a form I must fill out."

"That's normal. Let's get it done quickly. She needs an adult female friend, she can trust. Thanks for everything by the way."

"I am happy to help. I wish I could do more for her."

CHAPTER FIFTY

Powell used the phone he had taken from Manners to text Crawford. He sent a simple message;

"I need to meet you urgently. Somewhere central like Leicester Square would be best."

The reply came back quickly;

"OK. Can do 6pm tonight. There's a Mexican restaurant next to the Odeon cinema on Leicester square."

Powell felt a knot in his stomach as he read the reply. The arrogant git was suggesting meeting at the same place where he'd met Powell previously. Crawford had detonated the bomb that killed Lara while standing out front of the restaurant.

Powell felt decidedly uncomfortable as he arrived at the restaurant. Powell didn't enter the restaurant but walked to the nearby cinema and purchased a ticket to one of the films that had already started.

Powell had wanted revenge but with Crawford thrown out of the country, he had never believed he would get the chance. Perhaps that was why he had helped Alex gain retribution for what happened to her brother. Powell understood the need for revenge. It was a fire that burned strongly and wasn't easily extinguished. Sometimes it was necessary to act outside the law to obtain justice. Alex's execution of Bob had undoubtedly saved further children from experiencing the horror of his acquaintance.

Now Powell was ready to deal with his own demons. Despite what he intellectually knew to be the truth, he still felt guilty about Lara's death. In a permanent fight between his brain and his emotions, his emotions were often winning. The fact Crawford was still alive and plotting was an insult to her memory.

On a practical level, Powell didn't fancy spending the rest of his life looking over his shoulder. He was certain Crawford wasn't the type of man to forgive and forget. Somehow, Crawford would try again to get to Powell or those he loved. In the process, there was always a high risk of innocent people being killed. Crawford had to be stopped and it seemed unlikely the authorities would act. Despite not wanting to become a vigilante, Powell could not sit by and do nothing.

Powell had the weapon he took from Manners in his pocket. It would still have Manners' fingerprints all over it. Powell was wearing thin gloves and had been careful handling the gun. At the very least it might provide Manners with some difficult questions to answer. At best he might be charged with murder. If the authorities started looking into the relationship between Manners and Crawford, there would probably be further evidence of unsanctioned actions. It would all be covered up but it would leave Powell in the clear.

Powell had been careful when phoning Brian, to be on record pushing for Crawford to be kicked out of the country. He hadn't sounded like someone about to exact personal revenge. Not that Brian would reveal the detail of their phone calls but the Director General might decide to check up on Brian's conversations, which were all recorded.

Powell waited until closer to the meeting time and then left his seat to go to the foyer and buy a coffee. He typed a message to Crawford;

"Spotted someone I know near the restaurant. I don't want to be seen with you so I've dived in the cinema and bought a ticket to The Accountant. I'm in the back row on the left. Place is empty. Grab me a Latte. Thanks."

The layout of the screen meant anyone entering had to walk down the right hand side to the front when they entered and then walk up steps to sit at the back. Powell returned to his seat on the right about ten rows from the front. The cinema was dark as the film had been playing for some time. It's early start had also ensured there were only a handful of people watching he film.

It was ten minutes later when Powell spotted Crawford arrive holding the two cups of coffee. He stood for a second to get his bearings and then identified the man sitting by himself in the back row. Powell was fairly certain at a distance in the dark, Jenkins had a similar outline to Manners.

Crawford climbed the steps and passed Powell without a glance as his head was buried in Afina's neck. The cinema was large and each row of seats lengthy. It would take Crawford some time to get to the end of the row and realise it wasn't Manners.

Powell waited until Crawford was almost at the top of the steps before getting up from his seat. He moved quickly up the steps carrying the coffee in his left hand. If Crawford did turn around, Powell hoped he looked like an innocent cinema goer.

Crawford was making his way along the rear row of empty seats carrying the two cups of coffee, which if he was armed would make it impossible to reach quickly for a weapon.

Powell had moved quickly on the balls of his feet and was about ten seats away from Crawford, when he must have sensed danger and turned around. It was too dark for visual recognition but Crawford could see he was potentially trapped between two people.

Crawford dropped the coffees like hot bricks and reached for his gun. Powell's foot shot out and connected with Crawford's jaw, sending him spinning back onto the floor between the two rows of seats. In the confined space, Crawford tried to get his weapon out but Powell was on him too quickly.

In a movie, Powell would have made sure Crawford could recognise the man responsible for his death. The camera would have shown Crawford's look of horror in close up. But this was real life and Powell didn't waste a second. He stood over Crawford and put two bullets into his heart. Manners had been very thoughtful in having a silencer on his gun.

Jenkins was on his feet and helped Powell pick up Crawford's lifeless body, forcing him into the corner seat, resting his head against the wall. No one seemed to pay them any attention.

Satisfied Crawford looked as if he was sleeping, they hurriedly walked back along the row of seats and collected Afina. Powell walked out the cinema with his arm around Afina, looking like any loved up couple. Jenkins followed at a discrete distance behind.

Immediately outside the cinema was a large bin. Powell tossed the gun inside. If the police were thorough they would discover the murder weapon. But once the identity of Crawford was discovered, Powell hoped the Security Services would take over and close down the investigation.

EPILOGUE

Powell had been unexpectedly summonsed to a meeting with the Director General of the Security Services. Brian had no further information regarding the meeting and it was with some trepidation Powell waited outside the DG's office. It had been six weeks since the death of Crawford.

"The Director General will see you now," the woman sat at the desk outside his office announced, as if she could somehow read the DG's mind. In reality a discrete light had flashed on her desk.

The DG was standing as Powell entered and they shook hands. Powell was very pleased to see the DG was alone. He had been concerned Manners might be present.

"Have a chair," the DG said, indicating the round meeting table and four chairs.

Powell thought it positive they were going to sit at the meeting table rather than either side of the DG's massive desk.

"Well Powell, I hope we won't be having many more of these meetings. I can't deny your heart is in the right place but you do leave the most damnable messes for us to clean up after you."

Powell remained silent but raised his eyebrows.

"Fortunately," the DG continued. "Your actions also prove beneficial to the Service."

"I'm not really following you?" Powell replied.

"A camera outside Leicester Square tube station identified you as being in the area at the same time Crawford was killed."

"That's just a coincidence."

"Please spare me any bullshit. Nothing said between us will be repeated outside these walls. Crawford's death is no loss. He carried out acts of terrorism on our shores. What does intrigue me is how you came to be in possession of Ed Manners' gun, which you used to shoot Crawford."

Powell decided honesty was the best policy. "It's a long story. The short version is I took the gun from Manners when he was trying to shoot me."

"It was you who put him in hospital?"

"Yes."

"You do have a way of making enemies, Powell. Tell me why Ed was trying to shoot you."

Powell chose his words carefully. "I was bodyguard to Bob Hale. He was best friends with Jack Street, who was friends with Ed Manners."

The DG digested what he'd been told. "The same Jack Street, who featured so prominently on that vile video?"

"The very same."

"The same Bob Hale, who committed suicide while on drugs?"

"That's him."

"How do you know Manners was friends with those two?"

"I saw them together at Jack Street's house."

"Was that when Ed tried to shoot you?"

"Yes."

"You saw something you shouldn't?"

"Yes."

The DG again digested what he was hearing. "Are there any more videos anywhere?"

"Not to my knowledge."

"I have two girls at university. If I suspected someone of harming them in the way Street hurt that girl on the video, I would have no hesitation in ending his life."

Powell felt free to vent his real feelings. "All three men are the epitome of evil. Bob Hale paid the price for a crime he committed twenty years ago. Street is destroyed for what you saw in the video but that was the tip of the iceberg. Manners is equally as bad but I didn't have proof I could use. I'm sure it was Manners who pointed

Crawford and his team in my direction."

"So you planted the gun, hoping he would be picked up for Crawford's murder."

Powell didn't plan to make a direct admission to killing Crawford. "That makes an interesting hypothesis."

"Ed Manners is a senior and key member of my counter terrorism team. He won't be easy to replace."

"The longer you keep him in place, the greater the risk his activities will embarrass the Service and you personally."

"What do you take me for?" the DG snapped. "I don't give a damn about being embarrassed. I care about what he is doing to young children."

"Leopards can't change their spots. He won't stop."

"I will have some discrete enquiries made into his private life. I think it highly likely we will find something incriminating on his home computer."

"I think that would be for the best."

The DG stood up, signalling the meeting was at an end. "Take care, Powell. Try to stay out of trouble." He extended his hand for Powell to shake. "You know, if you ever fancy returning to work for us, I think we could find you a suitable position."

THE END

TRAFFICKING
Powell Book 1

Trafficking is big business and those involved show no remorse, have no mercy, only a deadly intent to protect their income.

Afina is a young Romanian girl with high expectations when she arrives in Brighton but she has been tricked and there is no job, only a life as a sex slave.

Facing a desperate future, Afina tries to escape and a young female police officer, who comes to her aid, is stabbed.

Powell's life has been torn apart for the second time and he is determined to find the man responsible for his daughter's death.

Action, violence and sex abound in this taut thriller about one of today's worst crimes.

5* Reviews

"This book is not for the faint hearted but it is a brilliant read."

"Keeps you at the edge of your seat throughout."

"Exciting, terrifying, brilliant."

"One of the best books I have read in a long time!"

"Will leave you breathless."

ABDUCTED
Powell Book 2

Powell returns in an action packed novel of violence, sex and betrayal!

He is trying to recover two children from Saudi Arabia, who have been abducted by their father.

In a culture where women are second class citizens, a woman holds the key to the success or failure of his mission.

Meanwhile, back in Brighton, Afina is trying to deal with a new threat from Romanian gangsters.

From the streets of Brighton to Riyadh, Powell must take the law into his own hands, to help the innocent.

5* Reviews

"Trafficking was masterful and this one is even better."

"Great thriller."

"Fabulous twists and turns."

"Strong, interesting characters."

DECEPTION
Powell Book 3

POWELL IS BACK IN A HEART POUNDING STORY THAT WILL LEAVE YOU BREATHLESS.

The Americans aren't happy with the changing political climate in Britain. Elements of the CIA and MI6 enter into a conspiracy to help shape the thinking of the British public.

Meanwhile ISIS has a plan to bring terror to the streets of Britain.

Powell is caught in the middle when he offers help to a former lover, whose life is in danger. Soon it becomes evident, someone will stop at nothing to see them both silenced.

Unsure who can be trusted, Powell must act to save the lives of his friends and right a terrible wrong.

5* Reviews

"Couldn't put the book down it was so gripping."

"Brilliant, like his other books, can't wait for his next book.."

"A thrill on every page."

BETRAYED
Powell Book 4

Powell returns in an action packed story of a commune, drugs and corrupt police officers.

Scott, the charismatic leader of the commune, promotes free love and the sharing of wealth.

Hattie is a twenty year old about to inherit a £25m fortune and her parents are worried about the influence Scott exerts on their impressionable daughter. Family ties will be tested to the limits.

Powell is hired to infiltrate the commune but finds himself framed for murder and on the run. Tired of being on the back foot he decides it is time to go on the offensive.

Betrayal is rife and sometimes from the most unexpected quarters.

5* Reviews

"Powell is becoming one of my favourite characters. Always a gripping read with lots of suspense."

"Fans of suspense, edge of your seat, fast-paced action thrillers should read this book and the other four."

"Another superb read from Bill Ward."

"I have really enjoyed the Powell series books. I haven't been able to put them down."

REVENGE.

There is no greater motivator for evil than a huge sense of injustice!

Tom Ashdown, an unlikely hero, owns a betting shop in Brighton and gambles with his life when he stumbles across an attempted kidnapping, which leaves him entangled in a dangerous chain of events involving the IRA, a sister seeking revenge for the death of her brother and an informer in MI5 with a secret in his past.

Revenge is a fast paced thriller, with twists and turns at every step.

In a thrilling and violent climax everyone is intent on some form of revenge.

5* Reviews

"Fast paced from the start and it only goes faster!"

"This novel is a real page turner!"

"It will keep you on the edge of your seat."

"Revenge is an example of everything that I look for in an action thriller."

ENCRYPTION.

In a small software engineering company in England, a game changing algorithm for encrypting data has been invented, which will have far reaching consequences for the fight against terrorism.

The Security Services of the UK, USA and China all want to control the new software.

The Financial Director has been murdered and his widow turns to her brother-in-law to help discover the truth. But he soon finds himself framed for his brother's murder.

When the full force of government is brought to bear on one family, they seem to face impossible odds. Is it an abuse of power or does the end justify the means?

Only one man can find the answers but he is being hunted by the same people he once called friends and colleagues.

5* Reviews

"A Great English Spy Thriller."

"This is a great story! Once I started reading it, I could not put it down."

"Full of memorable characters and enough twists and turns to impress all diehard thriller junkies, it is a wonderful read"

"If you're a fan of Ludlum, and love descriptive prose like that of Michener, you'll be right at home."

ABOUT THE AUTHOR

Bill Ward has recently moved from Brighton and now lives in Nottingham with his German partner Anja. He has retired from senior corporate roles in large IT companies and is now following a lifelong passion for writing! With 7 daughters, a son, stepson, 2 horses, a dog and 2 cats, life is always busy!

Bill's other great passion is supporting West Bromwich Albion, which he has been doing for more than 50 years!

Connect with Bill online:

Twitter: http://twitter.com/billward10bill

Facebook: http://facebook.com/billwardbooks

Printed in Great Britain
by Amazon

39977828R00115